Hell's Legionnaire

SELECTED FICTION WORKS BY L. RON HUBBARD

FANTASY
The Case of the Friendly Corpse

Death's Deputy

Fear

The Ghoul

The Indigestible Triton

Slaves of Sleep & The Masters of Sleep

Typewriter in the Sky

The Ultimate Adventure

SCIENCE FICTION
Battlefield Earth

The Conquest of Space

The End Is Not Yet

Final Blackout

The Kilkenny Cats

The Kingslayer

The Mission Earth Dekalogy*

Ole Doc Methuselah

To the Stars

ADVENTURE
The Hell Job series

WESTERN
Buckskin Brigades

Empty Saddles

Guns of Mark Jardine

Hot Lead Payoff

A full list of L. Ron Hubbard's
novellas and short stories is provided at the back.

*Dekalogy—a group of ten volumes

L. RON HUBBARD

Hell's
Legionnaire

GALAXY
PRESS

Published by
Galaxy Press, LLC
7051 Hollywood Boulevard, Suite 200
Hollywood, CA 90028

Printed in the United States of America.

ISBN-10 1-59212-355-4
ISBN-13 978-1-59212-355-1

Library of Congress Control Number: 2007903536

Contents

FOREWORD   vii

HELL'S LEGIONNAIRE   1

THE BARBARIANS   23

THE SQUAD THAT
NEVER CAME BACK   51

STORY PREVIEW:
WHILE BUGLES BLOW!   101

GLOSSARY   111

L. RON HUBBARD
IN THE GOLDEN AGE
OF PULP FICTION   121

THE STORIES FROM THE
GOLDEN AGE   133

Stories from Pulp Fiction's Golden Age

A ND it *was* a golden age.

The 1930s and 1940s were a vibrant, seminal time for a gigantic audience of eager readers, probably the largest per capita audience of readers in American history. The magazine racks were chock-full of publications with ragged trims, garish cover art, cheap brown pulp paper, low cover prices—and the most excitement you could hold in your hands.

"Pulp" magazines, named for their rough-cut, pulpwood paper, were a vehicle for more amazing tales than Scheherazade could have told in a million and one nights. Set apart from higher-class "slick" magazines, printed on fancy glossy paper with quality artwork and superior production values, the pulps were for the "rest of us," adventure story after adventure story for people who liked to *read*. Pulp fiction authors were no-holds-barred entertainers—real storytellers. They were more interested in a thrilling plot twist, a horrific villain or a white-knuckle adventure than they were in lavish prose or convoluted metaphors.

The sheer volume of tales released during this wondrous golden age remains unmatched in any other period of literary history—hundreds of thousands of published stories in over nine hundred different magazines. Some titles lasted only an issue or two; many magazines succumbed to paper shortages during World War II, while others endured for decades yet. Pulp fiction remains as a treasure trove of stories you can read, stories you can love, stories you can remember. The stories were driven by plot and character, with grand heroes, terrible villains, beautiful damsels (often in distress), diabolical plots, amazing places, breathless romances. The readers wanted to be taken beyond the mundane, to live adventures far removed from their ordinary lives—and the pulps rarely failed to deliver.

In that regard, pulp fiction stands in the tradition of all memorable literature. For as history has shown, good stories are much more than fancy prose. William Shakespeare, Charles Dickens, Jules Verne, Alexandre Dumas—many of the greatest literary figures wrote their fiction for the readers, not simply literary colleagues and academic admirers. And writers for pulp magazines were no exception. These publications reached an audience that dwarfed the circulations of today's short story magazines. Issues of the pulps were scooped up and read by over thirty million avid readers each month.

Because pulp fiction writers were often paid no more than a cent a word, they had to become prolific or starve. They also had to write aggressively. As Richard Kyle, publisher and editor of *Argosy*, the first and most long-lived of the pulps, so pointedly explained: "The pulp magazine writers, the best of them, worked for markets that did not write for critics or attempt to satisfy timid advertisers. Not having to answer to anyone other than their readers, they wrote about human beings on the edges of the unknown, in those new lands the future would explore. They wrote for what we would become, not for what we had already been."

Some of the more lasting names that graced the pulps include H. P. Lovecraft, Edgar Rice Burroughs, Robert E. Howard, Max Brand, Louis L'Amour, Elmore Leonard, Dashiell Hammett, Raymond Chandler, Erle Stanley Gardner, John D. MacDonald, Ray Bradbury, Isaac Asimov, Robert Heinlein—and, of course, L. Ron Hubbard.

In a word, he was among the most prolific and popular writers of the era. He was also the most enduring—hence this series—and certainly among the most legendary. It all began only months after he first tried his hand at fiction, with L. Ron Hubbard tales appearing in *Thrilling Adventures, Argosy, Five-Novels Monthly, Detective Fiction Weekly, Top-Notch, Texas Ranger, War Birds, Western Stories,* even *Romantic Range.* He could write on any subject, in any genre, from jungle explorers to deep-sea divers, from G-men and gangsters, cowboys and flying aces to mountain climbers, hard-boiled detectives and spies. But he really began to shine when he turned his talent to science fiction and fantasy of which he authored nearly fifty novels or novelettes to forever change the shape of those genres.

Following in the tradition of such famed authors as Herman Melville, Mark Twain, Jack London and Ernest Hemingway, Ron Hubbard actually lived adventures that his own characters would have admired—as an ethnologist among primitive tribes, as prospector and engineer in hostile climes, as a captain of vessels on four oceans. He even wrote a series of articles for *Argosy*, called "Hell Job," in which he lived and told of the most dangerous professions a man could put his hand to.

Finally, and just for good measure, he was also an accomplished photographer, artist, filmmaker, musician and educator. But he was first and foremost a *writer*, and that's the L. Ron Hubbard we come to know through the pages of this volume.

This library of Stories from the Golden Age presents the best of L. Ron Hubbard's fiction from the heyday of storytelling, the Golden Age of the pulp magazines. In these eighty volumes, readers are treated to a full banquet of 153 stories, a kaleidoscope of tales representing every imaginable genre: science fiction, fantasy, western, mystery, thriller, horror, even romance—action of all kinds and in all places.

Because the pulps themselves were printed on such inexpensive paper with high acid content, issues were not meant to endure. As the years go by, the original issues of every pulp from *Argosy* through *Zeppelin Stories* continue crumbling into brittle, brown dust. This library preserves the L. Ron Hubbard tales from that era, presented with a distinctive look that brings back the nostalgic flavor of those times.

L. Ron Hubbard's Stories from the Golden Age has something for every taste, every reader. These tales will return you to a time when fiction was good clean entertainment and the most fun a kid could have on a rainy afternoon or the best thing an adult could enjoy after a long day at work.

Pick up a volume, and remember what reading is supposed to be all about. Remember curling up with a *great story.*

—Kevin J. Anderson

KEVIN J. ANDERSON *is the author of more than ninety critically acclaimed works of speculative fiction, including* The Saga of Seven Suns, *the continuation of the Dune Chronicles with Brian Herbert, and his* New York Times *bestselling novelization of L. Ron Hubbard's* Ai! Pedrito!

Hell's Legionnaire

Hell's Legionnaire

BEHIND them, the ambush was sprung with the speed of a steel bear trap. One moment the Moroccan sunlight was warm and peaceful upon this high pass of the Atlas Mountains. The next lashed the world with the sound of flaming Sniders and Mannlichers and flintlocks.

Gray and brown djellabas swirled behind protecting rocks. Bloodshot eyes stared down sights. Scorching lead reached in with hammers and battered out lives with the gruesome regularity of a ticking clock.

Ann Halliday's shrill scream of terror was lost in an ocean of erupting sound. Her terrified Moorish barb plunged under her, striving to dash through the jamming corridor of the peaks.

Horses fell, maimed and screaming. Men died before they could reach their holsters, much less their guns. The two auto-rifles in the vanguard had been jerked from their packs but now they were covered with dust and blood and their gunners stared with glazed, dead eyes at the enemy, the Berbers.

John Halliday, Ann's father, tried to ride back to her. Within five feet of her pony, he stiffened in his saddle, shot through the back. The next instant his face was torn away by a ricocheting slug. He pitched off at her feet.

Muskets and rifles rolled like kettledrums. Black powder

smoke drifted heavily above the pass, a shroud to temporarily mark the passing of twenty men.

A voice was bellowing orders in Shilha and, dying a shot at a time, the volleying finally ceased. Then there was only dust and smoke and the blood-drenched floor of the pass.

Two Berbers, blue eyes hard and metallic in the hoods of their djellabas, jerked Ann Halliday from her barb. She struggled, but their sinews were trained by lifetimes spent on the Atlas and she might as well have tried to break steel chains.

Her boots made swirls of dust as she attempted to impede their progress. Once she looked back and saw a Berber delivering the death stroke to a wounded expedition aide. She did not look back again.

The Berbers half lifted, half threw her to the saddle of a waiting horse. Other mountain men were coming up, their arms filled with plunder. As though in a nightmare, Ann saw them mount their ponies.

They filed down the pass, up a slope, and trotted toward a mountain peak which loomed brown and sullen before them. The rapidity of the events was too much for her. They dazed her and made her slightly ill. But she had not yet realized that her party had been slain, that she was in the hands of revolting tribesmen. Mercifully, a sort of anesthetic had her in its grip.

Almost before she realized they were on their way, they stopped. Teeth flashed in laughter. Men were patting rifles and ammunition and bulky sacks of loot. Some of them pointed to her and laughed more loudly. She did not understand, not yet.

She did not struggle when they led her to the square block

of a house. She thought that within she might have time to rest and collect herself, that she might be able to devise some means of escape. But when the cool interior surrounded her, she stared across the room and knew that her experience had not yet begun.

A Berber was sitting there, knees drawn up, djellaba hood thrown back. His eyes were gray and ugly. His cheeks were thin and his strong arms were bundles of muscle as he extended them before him. He was white, true, and his hair and beard were brown. But from him there exuded a web of evil, almost tangible in its strength.

"Get thee from me!" snapped the crouching one to her two guards. They went without a backward glance, doubtless glad to be free and able to take their part in the loot division.

The bearded one on the mat looked appraisingly at Ann. He saw her delicate face, her full lips, her dark blue eyes. His study swept down. She was clothed in a cool, thin dress which clung tightly to her beautifully molded body.

Her breasts were firm and tight against the cloth. The material clung to her thighs, outlining smooth, mysteriously stirring indentations and curves.

The Berber licked thin lips, scarcely visible through the thickness of his beard. His eyes came back with a jerk to her face.

"I," he said slowly, "am Abd el Malek, the man who shall soon sweep the *Franzawi* from the plains and mountains of Morocco." His French was flawless. "I wonder that they did not kill you, but now . . ." He let his metallic eyes linger on her thighs. "Now I am overjoyed that they did not."

She threw back her head, her eyes alight with anger: "Abd el Malek, dubbed 'The Killer.' It might please you to know that I am not a *Franzawi*. I am an American and if anything should happen to me . . . I suppose you think you can wipe out an expedition and fail to have *la Légion* after you."

"*La Légion!*" He spat as though the name tasted bad. "What do I care about *la Légion*? There is no company within five days' march. Resign yourself, my little one, to the time you pass with me."

Her eyes lost a little of their rage. Something of terror began to creep into them. "But . . . but there might be . . . ransom."

"Ha! Ransom! What do I care for ransom? In my stronghold over the Atlas I have the price to buy every man, woman and child in Morocco. No, sweet morsel, I am not interested in ransom. Ordinarily I would not be interested in you, Christian dog that you are. I would not touch you."

He stood up, towering over her. She backed up against the mud wall.

"No," he said, "I would not be interested. But this campaign has been long, rather boring. My women are far away, and . . ." He smiled, fastening his hot eyes on her body.

Reaching out he tried to hold her wrist. She jerked it away and aimed a slap at his leathery cheek. He laughed, displaying discolored, uneven teeth. "So," he said, "you will have it another way."

He stripped a bundle of thongs from the wall. Taking one, he wheeled on her and, before she could dodge, he had placed his arm about her shoulders, holding her there powerless. She strived to writhe out of the grip, but he held her as though she had not moved. His fingers stroked her body and he laughed.

Taking the thong, he wrapped it quickly about her hands. Throwing it over a beam, he pulled it taut and lashed it there. She was held rigidly upright, unable to move. Her trimly shod feet barely touched the floor as she swung. Her brown hair cascaded down over her shoulders.

Languidly, as though this was something to be mouthed and enjoyed like a morsel of food too good to swallow, he reached up to the throat of her dress.

He brought his hand down with a wrench. The frail cloth ripped with a loud, rasping sound. Most of the dress fell in shreds on the floor.

Then, seizing a crude riding whip, he commenced to lash her body with all the lustful, sadistic passion one finds in the Riffs, the Berbers and the Jebel Druses—a lust to slay, to punish.

Ann threatened him, insulted him, but did not plead for mercy. As a member of a geographical expedition she had been in tight places before and knew that whining was not a way out of this predicament. Besides, she knew only too well that the agony she was undergoing was but child's play compared to the unspeakable mutilations and tortures inflicted by the desert women on deserters or captured prisoners of the Foreign Legion.

Suddenly he reached up and crushed her swinging body to him. The djellaba was like sandpaper against her skin. His beard was so many copper wires. She watched with horror-arrested eyes, her throat too tight to loose a scream.

7

Then, seizing a crude riding whip, he commenced to lash her body with all the lustful, sadistic passion one finds in the Riffs, the Berbers and the Jebel Druses—a lust to slay, to punish.

His hand was going up to the thongs. His hot foul breath beat in waves against her bosom. Abruptly, a Berber's scream pierced the hot dry air. The scream was followed by a rattle of machine-gun fire.

Head up, eyes eager, Ann Halliday listened. From close by came the staccato, stirring notes of a bugle sounding the charge. *La Légion!* The racketing snarl of an auto-rifle hammered the compound. Slugs, maimed by rocks, shrilled as they twisted through the air.

The babble of Berber voices was shrill. A face jutted through the doorway.

"La Légion!" shrieked the Berber. "Thousands of them! There is no escape!"

Abd el Malek's features were contorted with anger. He snatched a rifle from the wall and ran outside. The blast of the auto-rifle was quickening. A man fell in front of the door, digging agonized fingers into his waist.

Abd el Malek's shout was distinct above the others. "It is the vanguard! Mount! We still have time to escape!"

The crackle of Sniders and Mannlichers ceased but the auto-rifle raved on. The hard, heat-caked earth was hammered by the hoofs of departing horses. Another Berber dropped to the ground, choking and calling on Allah.

And then everything was quiet. The thin air of the Atlas was undisturbed beneath a spinning copper sun.

Boots were scraping the mud wall of the compound. Presently the regular steps of one man were audible.

Ann Halliday called out, "Over here! In this big hut!" Then, paradoxically, she wished she hadn't spoken. Here she was nearly naked, hanging by her wrists from a beam. And one had heard things about Legionnaires. . . .

A lean, tanned, handsome face appeared in the entrance. Keen gray eyes opened wide with surprise under the Legion kepi. The man came forward, mute with astonishment.

His eyes traveled over her body. He swallowed hard and reached for his tri-bladed bayonet. "I'm sorry," he said in English. "I don't mean to stare . . . stare at you . . . but . . . God, lady, but you're beautiful!" His eyes went hard after that. Hard and impersonal. He cut the thongs and she slumped into a sitting posture on the floor.

He eyed the remnants of her dress and then went outside. In a moment he was back, bringing some white garments—white except for the place a bullet had passed. There, they were red.

"I'm sorry, miss," said the Legionnaire. "I guess you'll have to wear this djellaba. The rest of the clothes are pretty fresh and clean. I found them in that dead . . . pardon me . . . in that Berber's pack."

Turning away from him, she slipped into the baggy garments and flung the cloak about her slim shoulders. Then, although she was white of face and weak from reaction, she smiled.

"You're American," she said.

"Yes. American. Come on. We'll have to get out of here before they come back. They'll stop running in a minute and . . ."

"But where are the rest of you? The rest of your outfit, I mean?"

"Outfit?" He stared at her blankly. "Miss, I haven't any outfit. Not any more, that is."

10

"And what does that mean?"

He glanced uneasily toward the distant trail and then turned again to her. "I'm . . . well, ma'am, I'm a deserter, I guess. I've been gone for twelve days."

"But you mean you drove them off by yourself?"

He grinned, his tan face growing a little red. "Yes, I guess that's right. You see, ma'am, I took this bugle and this auto-rifle when I left. That's all I'm carrying. Those and bullets. I have to travel fast. These hills are dangerous and then . . . well, there's a price on my head, you see. I . . . I killed a corporal back there at the post. He was going to shoot me and . . . well, I killed him.

"Right now, ma'am, we'd better get going. They're liable to come back. I'm trying to make Casablanca and the Atlantic."

"But how?"

"I heard the firing about three miles away from the pass and I went over and found a lot of dead men. Thinking they might have taken some captives, I came up to look into the matter. They thought . . ." he grinned again, more easily. "I guess they thought I was a whole regiment."

"But who are you?"

"I was John Doe of the Legion, ma'am. But if I'm caught I'll be John Doe of the *bataillon pénal*. My real name is Colton, ma'am. Dusty Colton. Let's get going. They left a couple horses over there."

She followed him across the body-strewn compound, the hot sun beating down upon her back. He held a barb for her and eased her up into the saddle.

A yell of rage and exultation came from the higher reaches

11

of the trail. Looking back, Ann saw the swirling robes of the riders sweeping down upon them. The Berbers were some five hundred yards away, riding hard. They had discovered the trick, and Abd el Malek was burning with two distinct fires. He had temporarily forgotten one of them in the suddenness of the attack, but he remembered it now.

Dusty Colton's barb plunged down a steep slope and veered sharply into the ravine. Hard on his heels came Ann Halliday, swinging low in her saddle, glancing back.

Spiteful puffs of dust were geysering about them. The Berbers were shooting from their saddles—picturesque but rarely accurate. If these men had been Arabs, thought Ann, the story would be different. A Berber is not exactly at home in the saddle.

Colton lashed his pony up a steep slope. The barb struggled, dust rising about its hoofs. Ann's mount sidestepped the boulders, and under the pressure of whip and rein, labored in the wake of Colton.

The Berbers still on the level, swung closer. Some of them dropped to the sand, kneeling to fire. A leaden slug smashed the leather of Ann's cantle. Another twitched her djellaba. Colton looked back through the suffocating haze and gave her a reassuring grin.

Colton's khaki blended well with the dry tan fog. His blond hair streamed out from under his kepi.

The Berbers were toiling up the slope behind them. The marksmen were trying their best to bring the horses down. Ahead was a ridge, and beyond it lay temporary safety . . . perhaps.

Ann's pony stumbled as a rock rolled under its hoofs. She stared up at the hogback. If they didn't reach it in another half minute, the marksmen below . . .

It was too steep for the barbs. Colton swung down and tugged at the reins. Ann swung out of the saddle and by utilizing all the strength in her slender body, managed to aid the slipping horse toward the ridge top.

Later, a bullet slammed into rock beside her and she dodged. She knew it was useless to dodge. You never heard the bullet that hit you.

Colton disappeared. His face came back in an instant over the top of the ridge. He yanked her up and shoved the pony into the shelter of a boulder. The auto-rifle was in Colton's hands.

"Don't look!" he ordered.

But she couldn't help but look. The auto-rifle started up like a triphammer. The Berber horsemen on the slope were cornered. One after another they fell, an avalanche of dead bodies and dust and tumbling rocks.

The marksmen at the base screamed and sought cover. A handful of them made it.

Colton stopped firing, looking steadily down at the havoc he had brought. "I guess," he said, "that that will hold them back for a little while."

"Did . . . did you get Abd el Malek? The leader?"

Colton snorted and rolled himself a cigarette from black tobacco. "Don't be foolish, ma'am. That coyote isn't going to expose himself any more than he can help."

She looked at his damply clinging shirt, noting the enormous strength which it concealed. He was handsome in profile, this Colton.

He looked at her sideways. "We'll stay for a minute and see to it that they don't try it again. We're not rid of them." Once more he looked at her. "Ma'am," he said, hesitantly, "do you happen to have any money?" Then he laughed at his own question. She couldn't have—not the way he had found her.

"Why money?"

His laugh was erased. "Why, ma'am, it takes money to buy your way out of Casablanca. I know some fellows there and it would be easy. . . . But it takes the dough, get me? The filthy lucre."

"I have some money in the Fez bank."

"Then you can forget about it. You'll be officially dead."

"Dead?"

"Sure. I can't turn you over or let you run the risk of going back alone. There's a price on my head. These Berbers want me bad enough, even though I was just a private. The Legion wants me worse than the Berbers. The *bataillon pénal* . . . Well, you just don't get discharged from the *bataillon pénal*."

"Money," she murmured, thinking. The hood of the djellaba almost concealed her face, but where the loose shirt parted at the throat, the beginning of . . . Colton jerked his face away and looked over the edge of the ridge.

"Listen," said Ann. "I know this sounds silly and all that, but there's only one place I can think of which would have money."

"And where's that?"

"In . . . you'll laugh at me. In the village of Abd el Malek!"

He did laugh. Recklessly. His fine teeth flashed in the sun and he pushed his kepi back away from his eyes. "*Sīdī*, you would make a fit mate for Hell's Legionnaire." Instantly the grin vanished. "I beg your pardon, ma'am. I didn't mean disrespect."

"Hell's Legionnaire? Why that?"

"They called me that in the company. They couldn't understand why I never had anything to do with women or liquor. They thought the devil was saving me for some vast purpose."

"Why didn't you . . . didn't you take on liquor and women?"

He stared at her and then relaxed. "A girl in Saint Louis said she loved me once. I loved her—or thought I did. She double-crossed me . . . It's an old story, why go on?" He fired a burst from the gun as a warning to those below.

Turning again, he said, "Abd el Malek's village, eh? Well, ma'am, I guess we'll just have to go down there and get the dough. You don't buy boat tickets with air."

He slid down to the waiting horses and helped her mount once more. After that they rode through an unending sea of brown mountains, hot dry dust, looming boulders.

Eyes keenly alert for suspicious movements anywhere, he doubled their trail—confusing it. He twisted and turned through the ravines which lay like black gashes through the mountains. He seemed to know where he was going, thought Ann.

Darkness overtook them beside a pool of spring water where the grass grew deep and cool. He tethered the horses, laid the gun down over a boulder where it would command the trail, and then pulled some squares of bitter chocolate from his shirt pocket. Passing the biggest piece to Ann, he ate silently.

With the going of the sun, a cold wind sprang up, incongruously chill after the 110 degrees of the day. Ann hunched down, folding the cloak tightly about her.

Across the pool from her, the Legionnaire stretched in the grass, pillowing his head on his pack. He lay there so quietly that she thought he must be asleep.

It grew even colder. The night was filled with the strange sounds of birds and the faraway calls of mountain cats. Ann shivered and looked through the chilly darkness at Colton's shadowy body. She thought time and again that she heard hoofs drumming up the dark trail.

At last she could stand it no longer. Crawling on her hands and knees she approached him. Her fingers found his arm and stayed there. He did not move. She crept in close to him, lying at full length. His body was warm. His face was a white blur six inches above hers. She snuggled closer, feeling security and companionship flood through her. She thought he still slept.

His arm moved easily and he drew her closer to him. His face came slowly toward her own. Her heart pounded with a sudden, great joy.

Abruptly he jerked his head back to the pack. His hands moved up to her shoulders and stayed there. In the darkness she could see that his jaw was set and hard. With a small sigh, she fell asleep, unheeding the night sounds of the Atlas.

Afternoon of the next day found them plodding through waves of suffocating heat. The mountains were thinning out and the air seemed to be more breathable. Grass was lusher and water ran in roistering streams toward the sea.

Mopping his damp brow, the Legionnaire turned to her. "We're almost there, ma'am. Abd el Malek's village is less than ten minutes' ride."

"But won't it be guarded?"

"Certainly. But the sun will be down in twenty minutes. And if Abd el Malek is away . . ."

"But if he's there before us?"

"What the hell, ma'am. We've got nothing to lose. That is, I haven't. Maybe you'd better stay behind in case . . ."

"I go where you do."

He shrugged. "If we're caught, it won't be pleasant watching me die. They'll gouge out my eyes and cut out my tongue. They'll lash me until I can't stand. . . . Pardon me, ma'am. I get used to talking about these things. And if they catch you . . ."

"I'm still going," she said, but her face was white and strained.

They dismounted and waited until the last shadows of the dying day stretched long across the valley. Colton went ahead after tethering their horses behind a boulder, out of sight.

The village came to them with astonishing rapidity. It had been around just two bends in the trail.

A dog barked, savagely. Lights glowed in two windows but no heads came forth to investigate the cause of the uproar. Cooking fires sent a haze of sweet-smelling smoke across the cleared space.

A man stood beside a boulder, staring out across the trail

17

and valley, rifle resting in the crook of his arm. A cigarette burned against his dark face, giving away his position.

Colton sidled up, shadow among shadows. His hand shot out like a pile driver. His other hand snatched at the sentry's throat. Ann heard a choking rattle. Colton shook the body, holding it up from the ground with one hand. When he dropped it, it sprawled as limp as an empty sack. The cigarette still glowed on the ground.

Coming back to Ann, Colton breathed, "That big house over there is Abd el Malek's. You stay outside and here's the sentry's rifle. If anything happens . . ." He shrugged.

Walking straight across the bare ground, Colton approached the large square hut with the lighted window. A horse was tethered at the entrance. That meant but one thing. Abd el Malek was there!

Without pausing, Colton walked straight through the entrance, auto-rifle held out before him like a lance.

The interior, smoky and poorly lit, was filled with mats and stacked guns. Two women stiffened against the far wall.

A man whirled about, his face drawn with surprise. It was Abd el Malek!

Colton's face was a dead mask. "One sound," he said in Shilha, "and this sprays death."

Abd el Malek sank back on the mat. His eyes had a searing quality as he stared up at the Legionnaire.

Colton wanted to laugh. It was too easy, this. One sentry and nothing else for protection. "I heard," said Colton, "that you had money."

Abd el Malek started. He involuntarily glanced toward a small cabinet at the far end of the room.

"So that's where it is," said Colton. "Thank you. I'm taking it in payment for the equipment and lives of the Halliday Expedition."

Abd el Malek chuckled. "You think you can do this, eh, Legionnaire? You think that one man is good enough? You have learned little with *la Légion*."

Edging along the wall, Colton approached the cabinet—out of place in this Berber scene. He reached down without taking his eyes from Abd el Malek. The door swung open. Several sacks came to view. Colton scooped them up with a single sweep of his hand and crammed them into his musette bag. They were heavy and jangling, those bags. God knew what wealth and loot they contained.

Suddenly the night was torn apart by a man's shout. Dogs began to bark hysterically.

They had found the sentry! Perhaps Ann!

Abd el Malek smiled. "Torture, Legionnaire, will be your lot. And worse if you fire that auto-rifle. We shall see to it that the woman is torn to pieces before your eyes—if the woman is still with you." He stood up, his gray eyes triumphant.

The women standing near, began to laugh with relief. Men were pounding toward the hut, calling out for Abd el Malek. Suddenly the doorway was filled with alarmed faces.

Colton glanced to the right and left. He was trapped and doomed. He had been a fool to try this. Why hadn't he let well enough alone? They knew he came to them singly now.

With only a woman to back him. They would find Ann and torture them both.

Abd el Malek was standing with folded arms. "Take away his plaything, my children."

Colton braced his back against the mud wall. "Try it." But he knew he was only prolonging things—that they would be harder on him if he resisted. He was whipped.

Berber hands were reaching out for the flared muzzle of the auto-rifle.

A shot rapped harshly through the gloom!

Abd el Malek weaved slightly. He took one step to the right, tried to stay on his feet. A red flood of frothy crimson bubbled from his thin lips.

In his eyes was the agony of death!

Colton stared, unbelieving. He could not understand. The Berbers were transfixed by the sight of their leader.

Hands flexing like talons, Abd el Malek went down on his knees. The flood of red doubled, trebled.

He coughed and fell on his face to lie quite still.

And then came the ragged notes of a bugle!

Colton caught his breath. *La Légion!* Then that meant the *bataillon pénal*—the Zephyrs for him. Colton, murderer and deserter.

But something in him wouldn't believe it. Something in him made him swing up the gun and fire—although Berber torture was nothing compared to the living death of the Zephyrs.

The auto-rifle spewed an unending stream of ragged flame. Berbers, swerving away too late, caught the bursts full in their chests. Colton strode forward to the door, his path cleared and carpeted by dying men. His face was set and hard.

Men streamed at him across the clearing. More Berbers. He fired the rest of the clip, replaced it, kneeling in the shadow of the wall.

Screams of terror and rage went up before him. The auto-rifle clattered on, punctuated by the bark of rifles. Slugs whined out across the darkness, bit into the running bodies and drove them to earth.

Ann's voice was in his ears. A pony's rein was in his hand. "Ride! Ride, for God's sake!"

And then he knew that she had blown the bugle and that she had killed Abd el Malek. For him? For herself? No, thought Colton, wind against his hot face, for both of them.

It was nearing dawn and the chill night was slowly ebbing away into faint yellowness in the east. Colton drew in and looked behind them and saw nothing. He smiled and pointed down to pinpoints of lights which glowed far below.

"Casablanca," he said.

"We've made it," murmured the girl, softly. "We've made it, you and I." And she sighed happily.

"We'll rest before we go on. There's a spring here. Yes," he said, dismounting, "we've made it and we've got God knows how many thousands of dollars in this musette bag. Enough to keep us the rest of our lives."

"Us?" she said, a little breathless.

He reached up to her and dragged her bodily out of the saddle. Pressing her against him, he nodded. "Us."

The Barbarians

The Barbarians

THE package arrived by native runner. Major Duprey, rotund and sleek in Foreign Legion khaki, eyed the thing distrustfully as it lay on his desk, struck by a beam of hot Moroccan sunlight. Not that he thought the package might explode before his face, but because the runner had come from Intelligence. Anything from Intelligence to the infantry was to be eyed—it usually meant the loss of a few men, a deal of worry.

The great square of Fez was visible through the open door of the whitewashed office—colorful, noisy, smelly, crammed with tribesmen down for the holiday. Ponies drooped sorrowfully in the rolling heat waves.

Major Duprey looked up from the package and stared at a man who approached the office. The man towered above the natives as a slender mountain peak towers above foothills.

"*Capitaine* Harvey!" bawled Duprey.

The tall man looked languidly toward the open door and then shoved his way toward it. He entered and sat down in a wicker chair, thrusting his booted legs out before him. He rolled a cigarette, twisted the end, placed it in his mouth. He spent almost a minute looking for a match as though unconscious of Duprey's glare. It was not until blue smoke rolled from Jack Harvey's cigarette that he glanced up inquiringly.

"*Capitaine!*" said Duprey, severely. "How often must I tell you that an officer of the Legion must not be seen in undress uniform in public? And how often must I remind you to wear a sun hat instead of that dirty white helmet? Besides, *Capitaine*, you have grease spots on your jacket and that white silk scarf about your throat is not regulation."

Jack Harvey lifted the flying helmet from his black hair and shoved it into his pocket. His sun-narrowed eyes, quite unperturbed, wandered out to the square once more. His face was long and drooping, the expression almost sad.

Duprey rubbed his hands together briskly. The two runners who sat against the far wall, dozing in the stuffy heat of the office, jerked up their heads, straightened their khaki shirts and generally began to look alive.

Duprey's nose wrinkled as though he had smelled something offensive. He glanced with long-suffering eyes at the square and then looked back at the cubical package. Once more he rubbed his hands and then untied the rope which held the paper in place.

Harvey watched him without interest.

The wrapping paper fell away like a banana skin and a box came to view. Once more Duprey paused to sniff. His attention was suddenly riveted to the package.

He struck away the cardboard and jumped back as though a snake had struck at him. One of the runners gagged. Harvey sat up straight, very alert and forgot the cigarette.

"*Mon Dieu!*" cried Duprey. "Look at that!"

There was no need for the order. All eyes were on the head. It was a terrifying thing, that head. Its ragged, severed throat was ringed by congealed blood. Its eyes had been gouged out. Small twigs had been thrust through the jaws, leaving jagged holes. The sightless sockets looked up at Duprey.

The runner gagged again and went to the door. Harvey swallowed twice, remembered his cigarette and took a drag from it. Duprey was pressed all the way back against the wall, as though the head had a gun trained on him.

"It's Grauer," Duprey said.

"Poor devil," said Harvey.

"And now," Duprey snapped somewhat irritably, "we'll get no further reports from the back country. The fool would have to get himself caught."

Harvey's eyes glinted.

"Yes," he said. "A personal insult to you, Major. Caid Kirzigh was trying to be funny."

"Caid Kirzigh," nodded Duprey, looking down at the tortured face. "The barbarian! I thank the good God that *I* belong to the civilized parts of the world. I'll show that one! I'll show him that he cannot flaunt our authority in this country."

"How?" said Harvey and was immediately sorry that he had spoken. The major's eyes were on him.

"How?" echoed Duprey. "We'll see to it that the Legion wipes him out, that's how. We'll storm his territory and teach them a lesson."

"Storm his stronghold? That would be about half of the Atlas, wouldn't it?"

"Half the Atlas, yes. But the caid is bound to be accessible.

27

He must be with one or another body of his troops. We'll strike and strike hard. Have to teach those barbarians a lesson. Can't let them get away with such brutality, with such insults to France." His eyes were once more on Harvey.

After a moment, the major said, "*Capitaine*. You will proceed immediately with a gunner to the higher reaches of the Atlas. You will land and scout Caid Kirzigh's position. Then you will return here and report."

"Major," replied Harvey, with great slowness, "I am perfectly willing to scout the position for you, but as for landing, the Atlas are not under your authority. And if I am caught . . ."

"You are impertinent," crackled Duprey. "Take a Caudron and make immediate reconnaissance. Land somewhere in the vicinity of . . . of . . ."

"Go ahead," smiled Harvey. "I'm listening."

Duprey struck the desk with his fist. The head jumped toward the edge, teetered there for an instant and then fell to the concrete floor.

Harvey winced. The jaw had fallen slack, displaying a blackened tongue and broken teeth. Duprey rounded the edge of the desk and scooped the thing up, putting it back in place. But as he did so something caught his eye.

Reaching into the mouth, he dragged forth a folded slip of yellow paper, damp with blood.

Unfolding the slip, he read it quickly. "Thoughtful of Grauer. Very thoughtful of him. He might know we would want this information."

To Harvey came the cold realization that Grauer must have known his fate long before it was meted out. He had written that message in his stolid German way, while he waited for his execution. And that Grauer had been told that his head would be shipped back to Fez.

"Kirzigh," said Duprey, "is about a hundred and fifty miles due south. He's holing in for a siege, putting up barricades about his towns, intending to attack and then retreat, leading our troops into ambush. He is now at village 8-G."

Harvey was staring at the place the head had been dented by the fall.

"*Capitaine,*" crackled Duprey. "You will go out to the drome immediately and take off. Do not fail to be back by morning with the required intelligence."

Harvey climbed to his feet. His long body was as lithe as a strip of whalebone. His sun-narrowed eyes seemed to sink into his long face. He swung a small stick back and forth. For a moment it appeared that he was about to object. Then he shrugged and went out of the office toward a waiting motorcycle.

Duprey was rubbing his hands, looking at the head. "The barbarians. I'll show them they can't insult *la Légion*! I'll show them, the filthy rabble!"

At the drome, with the heat waves rolling up from the hard-packed plain like dry steam, Harvey stopped before the hangars and beckoned to a sergeant.

"Rubio," said Harvey, listlessly, "tell them to run out a Caudron and gas her up."

Rubio's Spanish face gleamed. His bright, hard eyes glistened. "A patrol this time of day? *Sí, Capitaine.*"

"And Rubio," said Harvey, calling the man back, "are you doing anything tonight? Anything important?"

"Well, no, *Capitaine.*"

"All right, Rubio. You're going with me."

"But, *Capitaine . . .*"

"I said you were going with me," stated Harvey, swinging his small stick. He smiled wryly. "This, Rubio, is for France."

"To be sure, *Capitaine.* For France!"

The Caudron came forth, looming hugely before the hangar. The 450 hp Moraine-Ditrich motor thundered into uproarious life and the biplane quivered under the stress of cold cylinders. Looking at it, feeling the hot, dry sun against his shoulders, Harvey thought to himself that those frail wings alone would keep his head on his shoulders. A cigarette drooped from his lips and he squinted his eyes to see through the smoke.

The prop wash was a fog of tan, stinging particles which rose up to coat the world a drab monotone, matching the uniforms and faces of the men. Far, far off, almost against the feet of the looming High Atlas, there lay one patch of green. An olive orchard and vineyard. Harvey always circled it before he landed, thankful for a splash of color in a brown world. Morocco had little in common with Georgia. It was even more lifeless than those desert stretches of the Texas border where the customs patrol . . .

Rubio was climbing into the rear pit, swiveling the machine guns, making certain that the ordnance officer had been on the job. Rubio's glittery eyes were slightly worried.

The flaps of Harvey's helmet had been standing up like a police dog's ears. He pulled them down, fastened the buckle and folded the white scarf against his chest.

The Caudron rolled down the loose sand runway. The Moraine-Ditrich thundered. The spreading wings throbbed in the dead, rocky air, then they were soaring up against a metal blue sky and a copper sun.

The olive trees went under them slowly and then the ground began to inch up toward their spindly undercarriage—although the Caudron was climbing at a steep angle.

Harvey sat back and watched the High Atlas play the usual trick of receding as you approached. The black compass bowl swung back and forth, influenced by several billion tons of unexploited iron ore, which now served only one purpose: to throw troops off their route. A shadow fell across the instrument panel; the machine guns pointed west. Harvey used the shadow as a guide. A Legionnaire lost and downed in the Atlas was a dead Legionnaire.

Almost invisible, even in this hard, brilliant air, he could see Mt. Tizi-n-Tamjurt hundreds of miles away, fourteen thousand feet high. Looking back, he could have seen the Mediterranean, but he avoided that. Men sailed away from there via the sea.

The Caudron forged onward, higher and higher, reaching back into Berber country. Below, Moorish barbs toiled along a twisting road beneath the weight of native riders. One of the riders shook a rifle and his dark face opened to give vent to a challenging but unheard yell of defiance.

The machine guns racketed with harsh violence. Harvey jerked around to look at Rubio. The Spaniard was smiling as he swiveled the guns back, locking their butts.

Far below the man and the barb were struggling feebly in the hot, dry dust.

"For France," said Harvey to himself and flew steadily onward into thinning air.

The country was upended, twisted and gashed, offering only ravines and craggy cliffs in lieu of landing fields. An occasional ridge flattened out and ran crookedly for a space of a mile or more, to dip off into a gully and disappear.

When they made the world, thought Harvey, they took all the stones and rubbish which were left over and dumped them into northern Africa.

Rubio was slapping his helmet, pointing down. Harvey circled, one wing pointing steadily at the ground. Heat and wind lift combined in their effort to upset the ship. Rubio was pointing at a tight huddle of dirt houses. Down there men were running in circles, shouting, waving their guns.

Rubio cocked the machine guns and let drive. Small patches of gray white did not move again.

"The empire of Caid Kirzigh." Harvey told himself.

He flew on, deeper into the hills. His eyes raked the ground as he searched out the impossible—a landing field. He had been ordered to land and give the barbarians a lesson. Perhaps he could follow his orders.

Flying at half throttle, buffeted by blasting currents of rising air, he came back toward the village. Rubio was slapping his helmet again.

A canyon sliced a straight dark line across the world for almost two miles. It was not wide, never more than a hundred yards, and generally less by half. Boulders studded the flat floor. Harvey frowned and dived two hundred meters. Yes, there was one place where no boulder existed. A runway, about fifty yards wide and a thousand yards long.

Lift was careening up from the steep canyon sides. The altimeter needle was unable to react, seemingly paralyzed by the task of recording their rapidly varying height.

Harvey sent the Caudron toward the canyon end, did a wingover and came back. Cutting the Moraine-Ditrich down to idling, he shot toward the one cleared space. The roar of the engine was replaced by the shrill whistle of wires.

A bump struck their right wing. Harvey fought the stick and righted the plane. A heat area came under them and bounced them fifty feet before Harvey could once more nose down.

It was an atmospheric whirlpool, that spot. Harvey eyed the nearing sheer walls and saw them close in over the top of his head.

They rocketed for a cliff side. He banked and slammed the Caudron closer to earth. A boulder reached greedily at the right wheel and then whipped past.

The landing gear crunched. They rolled to a shuddering stop.

Rubio let go of the gunner's pit turtleback and climbed out. "Now what do we do?" he asked.

"Walk toward their camp, catch one of them and take him back with us."

"Yes, yes," said Rubio. "We'll get it out of them. . . ." He made a movement with his hands, pantomiming the throttling of a throat.

Harvey stepped to the wing and then to the ground. He lashed the heavy automatic down to his thigh, turning up his ear flaps to keep his neck cool, and walked toward the end of the ravine. Small geysers of dust came up from his boot heels.

When they could sight another canyon, Harvey stopped.

"They might be looking for us," he remarked.

"Those?" said Rubio. "The dirty beasts haven't got sense enough to get out of sight, much less look for us. Remember what happened down there at . . ."

Harvey nodded, taking a long drag at the smoke.

"For France," he said.

"For France!" echoed Rubio.

Harvey strode on toward the mouth of the second ravine. His eyes were alert for swirls of gray behind rocks, though he knew that their first warning of ambush would be the sharp whine of a maimed bullet turning over and over as it ricocheted from stone.

He loosened the automatic in its holster and laid back the flap. If they could just collar one of them and drag him back to the ship, everything would be set. But Berbers rarely travel alone and they rarely let you get within five hundred yards of them.

And five hundred yards across these ridges and canyons might as well be a thousand miles. Well, thought Harvey, it was a good idea anyway. After all, if Kirzigh got loose in the Legion outposts, a good many men would die.

Rubio was trotting along behind him, panting in the heat, his swarthy face greased with shining sweat.

Harvey stopped and looked at a wall two hundred yards away. Narrowing his eyes against the glare and shimmering heat waves, he stared intently. Yes, he was right. Someone had skipped from one boulder to another.

He went on toward the rock face as though he had seen nothing. Rubio, unknowing, followed hard on his heels.

Directly under the spot he had seen the movement, Harvey dived for the edge of the ravine. A bullet hit a rock with the spiteful sound of a broken banjo string.

Harvey scrambled up the steep slope toward a puff of dark smoke drifting languidly against the metal blue sky. A second bullet rapped shrilly and then a third.

The Berber was not only shooting at his enemy; he was also signaling the time-honored call of three. Bullets were far too precious to these Berbers. They even located spent French slugs after hours of search and remolded them.

Abruptly the down-slanting barrel of a Snider was above Harvey's head. He grabbed at the warm barrel and with a tendon-spraining wrench, brought it toward him, brought the Berber with it.

For one fast-moving second he thought he had succeeded, that this was a lone sentry who could be delivered for questioning.

And then swirls of dirty white sprouted from the barren

slopes of the ravine. Harvey, with his hands full of rifle and native, sent one hasty glance down at Rubio. And saw that Rubio was lost in a sea of whirling cloth.

Across Jack Harvey's vision there flashed the image of that head. That severed head with the eyeballs hanging by strings from the sockets. The head which had once rested on the stolid shoulders of Grauer.

Berbers came up the slope like an avalanche in reverse. Their scaly hands reached out as though already clutching the body of the *Franzawi*. Sniders, Mannlichers, flintlocks glittered in the hard sunlight. A howl came up from some hundred throats.

Harvey pulled his Berber down to him and threw the man headlong into the first wave. A small cluster of gray went spinning, skidding down the ravine, sending up a cloud of strangling dust.

The second wave drew back and dropped into the protection of boulders. After that only the black muzzles of rifles and the red-shot whites of eyes were visible.

Harvey took the automatic out of its holster and dropped it in the dust. They came up to him then, and took hold of his arms, leading him into the bottom of the canyon.

Rubio was swearing in a monotonous, high-pitched voice, trying to dash the blood out of his eyes so that he could see.

"Steady," said Harvey.

They were marched by a twisting route to the village. As Harvey listened and watched his triumphant foes, he was reminded of a parade through the streets of Rome, where the captives were lashed to chariot wheels, made to walk before the multitudes, led ignominiously, like beasts.

The tallest, broadest, whitest house in the village seemed to be their destination. Standing there on the heat-cracked earth was Caid Kirzigh.

He was bland, not at all fierce and scowling. His smooth cheeks were no darker than an Italian's; his beard was well combed. And his eyes were a light blue, suggesting Western ancestry. His burnoose was whiter than the rest and his hands were clean and soft. He was almost as tall as Jack Harvey though much older and therefore a little expansive about the belt line.

Harvey was thrust to the front, face to face with Kirzigh.

"*Franzawi*," said the caid, smiling a little, "we are glad to make you welcome."

Harvey looked at the blinded Rubio. "Like you made Grauer?"

There was no hostility to his voice. His tone merely suggested that it was rather hot to stand out here in the sunlight.

"Ah," replied the caid, "that was his name. I wondered if you had received my message." He smiled with assurance. He knew that his French was flawless. "Perhaps, when you flew overhead, if you had not taken it upon yourself to slaughter some dozen of my men and horses, I might even now greet you as a guest. However, your action and the attitude of my men will scarcely permit that."

"No, of course not," agreed Harvey.

"They are a little hard to hold, *Capitaine*. Like the men of your Legion at times, *hein*? The time the Legionnaires attacked that peaceful village south of here and killed the old men and . . . well, soldiers and women . . ."

"I don't recall," said Jack Harvey.

"Of course not. You do all your killing from the air, naturally. You do not know what happens here on the ground. You kill and fly away, *hein*?"

"Yes," Harvey replied. "Yes, of course."

"Ah, I see you are a man of understanding, *Capitaine*. But come, let us get on with this. My men have waited long for one of your sky birds to fall in their midst. Suppose we start with the sergeant, *hein*?"

"Torture?" said Harvey.

Caid Kirzigh turned and began to bawl orders in a language which Berbers will tell you is Shilha. The men about Rubio snatched heavy holds on his arms and lugged him, feet trailing in the dust, to a mud post in the center of the village.

Rubio was once more swearing—words picked up in the gutters of faraway towns. However, the Berbers did not understand.

Harvey looked on. He could do nothing else. Rifles were hard against his spine. His turn would come next.

Rubio was lashed to the post, arms extended. Unable to see, his imagination was gaining the upper hand over his sanity. He screamed an incoherent gibberish of French, Spanish and Italian. He kicked out with his legs until they fastened them down with leather thongs.

Caid Kirzigh looked at Harvey. "It may be a little brutal, but these men of mine—they have long memories."

A tall, withered man with a completely expressionless leather-face drew out a rough knife and tested its edge with a thick thumb. Evidently satisfied, he approached the writhing sergeant.

Harvey stiffened and the rifles bored deeper into his spine.

The leathery one reached up and ripped away Rubio's shirt, exposing the rippling muscles of the white back. With two quick slashes he drew the sign of the cross. The blood came slowly from the wounds. Rubio screamed louder.

Taking a handful of salt, the leathery one rubbed it into the slashes. Then he reached back for a whip, his fingers as thin and fleshless as so many stale bones.

The whip shrilled as it came down. It landed with a report as loud as any pistol shot. Harvey winced as though the lash had struck him. Rubio moaned with agony.

The whip came down again and then rose and fell so many times that Harvey lost count. Not that he was counting. He tried to look away, but each report brought his eyes swinging again to the bleeding pulp which was Rubio's back. The marks of the knife cross had long since disappeared in the presence of countless red-blue, oozing gashes.

Tired, the leathery one stopped and mopped the sweat from his forehead. He dropped the whip from his numbed hand and rubbed his tired muscles.

Rubio had sagged against the thongs. His head lolled crazily, loosely. His glazed eyes stared up unseeing at the metal blue sky.

A tall, withered man with a completely expressionless leather-face drew out a rough knife and tested its edge with a thick thumb.

The crowd turned sullenly to Jack Harvey. The caid shook his head at them and waved the guards toward the biggest, whitest square house.

The back of Harvey's shirt was blackened with sweat. He stumbled twice, groggy with heat and reaction.

Caid Kirzigh motioned that the *capitaine* should seat himself upon a mat in the dim interior. Harvey leaned back against the wall, eyed the caid.

Harvey could see the sagging body of Rubio through the doorless entrance.

"For France," he said quietly.

Caid Kirzigh had not heard. Rubbing his hands together he smiled. "*Capitaine,* I believe you left your plane nearby. Is that not so?"

"Yes, that's true."

"And hidden somewhere in that plane," said the caid, "you will have military maps of all Morocco, showing the railheads, the outposts, the concentration centers. Is that not so?"

"Maybe."

Kirzigh nodded brightly. "Then, perhaps if you were to show me these maps and tell me some other small things, I might . . ." He raised his hands in a vague gesture and leaned forward on his haunches. "I might see fit to let you off with mere shooting."

"You have large ambitions," said Harvey.

"Not too large. After all, *Capitaine,* we had all Europe in our power at one time, you know."

"Did you?"

"Ah, yes. The Moors, you see . . . Perhaps again . . . One

never knows these things until he sees the pages of the Great Book. We built all the structures which Spain considers so beautiful. We introduced an architecture that was new and still lasts. We invented the curved sword with which we captured the world. We invented the system of counting, the mathematics which you conquesting barbarians use to plot your artillery trajectories. Is it so strange that I should like to know about these maps?"

"You want to see the maps, that's all?"

"That's all. Just the maps. I should, of course, like to hear some other things, but . . ." He shrugged.

Harvey nodded. "All right. Perhaps you hold the winning cards, Kirzigh. I'll show you the maps if you'll . . . well, if you'll let me off with a mere shooting."

"Excellent," smiled the caid. He sprang up and went to the door. "We still have a little time before darkness. We shall go, *hein?*"

Jack Harvey stood up and allowed himself to be led into the fading sunlight.

It was still hot now, but later in the night it would grow cold—cold enough to make a man want blankets. Porous rock does not hold heat for long.

Accompanied by most of the men in the village, they trooped down the length of a ravine, avoiding boulders, climbing over obstructions. Two rifles were close to Harvey's shoulder blades, ready to blow him apart.

Caid Kirzigh was happy, joking with his men as he walked. Harvey listened to him, trying to piece together the drift of affairs.

Walking along the floor of another ravine, Harvey said, "Your plan, Kirzigh, would seem to be sound enough."

"Then you speak Arabic. I did not know."

"Not well, but enough. Your French, Kirzigh, is excellent."

"Ah, you like my French, *hein*? I spent enough time learning it. In Paris, you see. Among those *Franzawi* that came after the Moors had left."

"But don't you think," said Harvey, "that you're letting ambition run away from sense?"

"How do you mean?"

"This idea of wiping out the French. They have guns, planes, soldiers by the division. They'd stop you before you could start."

"Brains and the courage of my men will do it," said the caid. "Of course this matter will take considerable time. We will wipe them out, outpost by outpost, railhead by railhead. We have, *mon capitaine,* studied the methods evolved by the Englishman, Lawrence, and find them to be quite enough."

"But to think of . . ."

"Of a handful of tribesmen, *Capitaine,* growing into an avalanche of running horses, flaming guns, wiping the *Franzawi* from the face of the earth. And why not? They loot our villages. They take our women and cast them aside—dead. They destroy our crops. They interfere with our religion. Something must be done. It is not presumptuous to think that I am the man to do it. Careful preparation . . . You know, I am sure."

They had come into the ravine where the plane had landed. The Caudron spread its silent wings across the sand as though waiting for its master. Its shadow was long in the shaft of faded sun which came down to it.

Distrustful of the ship, the Berbers stopped a hundred paces in front of it, eyeing first the caid, then the wings. They had heard this thing snarl. They had seen death pour out from it. And nothing Caid Kirzigh could do would make the bulk of them continue on.

Kirzigh looked into the faces of his men and then shrugged.

"It is all right," he said. "You are within easy shot of a hundred good rifles. The three of us shall continue."

The three included one guard. The others hung back.

The tail of the plane was pointing toward them. Kirzigh, sword unsheathed, approached with sidelong glances at Harvey.

"Remember," said the caid, "that should you try to get into that ship and away they will riddle you with bullets. And if you are unlucky enough to be alive after such a move . . ."

Harvey strode on, the rifle probing into his spine. His face was quiet, composed. They reached the side of the fuselage and Harvey pointed into the rear pit. "The charts are there."

"I shall remove them," replied the caid. He rummaged through the interior, a little dazed by the presence of so many strange things. Presently, he backed away and pointed up. "You get them out."

Harvey grunted and climbed up over the rim. He dropped to the seat and fumbled under the panel.

Suddenly he straightened. Grabbing the butts of the twin guns he swiveled them around and down with one fast jerk.

The Berber rifle exploded almost against his waist. The slug whirled him, numbed him. He clawed at the butts, keeping his feet only through the force of will.

The machine guns racketed. The guard fell, hands extended. Kirzigh caught the burst in the chest and lower jaw.

Rifles hammered and the tribesmen began to surge forward. Harvey brought the guns about and pressed the trips. They leaped, quivering in his hands. Right to left, left to right. Six, seven hundred slugs a minute from each gun. The breech gnawed through the belt, spitting out empty, tinkling brass cases.

The Berbers stopped for an instant and then came on again. A bullet smashed its way through the flesh of Harvey's arm. The guns grew melting hot. The rush stopped once more. The men glanced fearfully about and found they stood in isolated groups. The red-tinged sand, fired by the dying sun, was clotted with unmoving bundles of white, strewn about like empty sacks.

With a concerted scream of terror, the tribesmen sprinted for the shelter of the canyon end. Harvey gave them three short bursts.

He did not know that he was badly hit. He was only thinking about the engine. Racing around to the front, he yanked through on the prop. Diving through the interwing section, he threw on both magnetos. Back at the prop again he found strength enough to pull it through. At any instant they might return.

The Moraine-Ditrich was faithful. It roared into chattering life, sucking flame into its water-cooled cylinders.

Stumbling, Harvey placed his hands on the cockpit rim. Looking down he saw Caid Kirzigh's head, blood-spattered and mangled against his dusty boots.

A tired frown flicked across the *capitaine*'s graying face. Looking down the ravine, he saw that the men had not had time to form another attack. He gripped the bright sword and, with a grunt of distaste, lopped off Kirzigh's head!

When the gory thing rolled free from the body, Harvey swallowed hard, a little sick. But it had been necessary. It was not until then that he noticed the guard striving to get at his fallen rifle.

Unmindful of his own weakness, Harvey threw both guard and head into the rear cockpit. The Berber slumped down, eyes glazed with terror.

The Caudron wallowed through the sand, picking up speed. Seeing it go, the Berbers turned and ran after it, shouting and waving their guns, pausing to fire. They stopped when they came to the headless body of their caid.

The motorcycle lurched to a stop before the door of the office on the great square of Fez. Two were riding in the side car and a Legionnaire was astride the saddle.

Capitaine Jack Harvey, shaky from exhaustion, lifted the dead weight of the Berber from him and stood up. He approached the square light which fell from Duprey's entrance, yellow on black stone.

Major Duprey whirled at the sound of boots, stopping midway in his restless stride down the concrete floor. Harvey was without tunic and his sleeve was rolled up to his shoulder, displaying bandages. He carried a red-smeared burnoose in his hand.

"You're late," said Duprey, glowering.

Harvey placed the bundle on Duprey's desk. "I was detained," he said slowly, "and Rubio is dead."

"Rubio? And who the devil is Rubio? What's this thing you've got here, man?"

"A souvenir," replied Harvey. His eyes were watchful, studying Duprey's face.

Duprey muttered something and then saw the Berber who was being held outside. "Who's that?"

"A man I captured. I believe it would be better, Major, to turn him in to the hospital. He's wounded."

"Wounded, you say? What do I care about a wounded Berber? He'll know all about the plans these barbarians have been concocting to launch against France. Gian!"

Gian, sleek as a staff officer should be, came out from an adjoining room, the picture of a perfect soldier.

"Gian," said Duprey. "Take that Berber out there and put him through the . . ."

"You mean . . . ?" said Gian.

"Information, understand? And it's no matter to us if you kill him. But get the information. Get it, do you hear?"

Gian saluted and went out. The Berber was led away. Duprey turned back to his desk and the bundle.

"Now," he said, "now let's see what you've got here."

He unfolded the smeared burnoose and disclosed the

bullet-mangled head of Caid Kirzigh. For a moment he was startled.

"It's Kirzigh's," supplied Harvey, still watchful.

"Kirzigh's. Ho! That's a joke. He sends me a head and then I have his. Well, that's fair enough, isn't it? Ugly-looking brute, wasn't he? These damn uncivilized devils think they're above losing their lives. Well, I showed them, didn't I?"

Harvey swallowed. His alert eyes grew a little haggard.

Duprey replaced the wrappings. "Kirzigh's head! Ah, that's the best joke yet. Here, I must take this over to the colonel. He'll be pleased, *Capitaine*, very pleased."

Duprey went briskly to the door, the grisly burden swinging carelessly at his side. He remembered something and turned. "Oh, yes, Harvey. I see you're wounded. Get it fixed up and turn yourself in to the hospital. You'll . . . well, you'll get a mention in the orders of the day for this. By the saints," he laughed, "you might even get a medal."

"For France," said Harvey, dully.

"For France!" cried the major. Night swallowed his footsteps.

Harvey went to the desk and picked up a bottle of cognac, pouring himself a stiff shot. He raised the glass to the height of his eyes and said, "For France," very quietly. Then he drank and limped out to the great square.

For half an hour he stood there, watching the natives pass back and forth. Watching their straight shoulders and observant blue eyes, their silks and fine leathers. For the first time, he was seeing them.

He sighed finally and turned to go toward the hospital. He felt disappointed, let down. Hollow inside, somehow, as though he had lost something which rightfully belonged to him.

But then, of course, you couldn't expect Major Duprey to get the point.

They were laughing in the colonel's quarters.

The Squad That Never Came Back

CHAPTER ONE

The Dying Man

B ACK in Sidi-bel-Abbès they still think that my squad and I died in a miserable outpost on the northern slope of the High Atlas Mountains. Well, they're seven-eighths right. I'm still living, but the rest of the squad have long since given their bones to dust in the rocky heights of Morocco. I could not go back until it was too late—and now I don't want to.

Besides, the papers tell me that they are thinking the Legion will be held only as a police force and labor outfit from now on. That lets me out.

The papers tell me other things. And one of these things has prompted me to write my story. The news concerns a discovery made in Morocco a short while back.

Two airmen, according to a press dispatch, were flying south of Casablanca over uncharted terrain. They brought back the tidings that they had discovered a city in a lake. Their guess was that it was an ancient Roman city, untouched for centuries.

Also, they are thinking of fitting out an expedition to visit that place overland. Judging from the reports of the two airmen, it would seem that the four corner towers and the wall are clearly visible in this lake.

That expedition is due for a surprise. They'll drain that

lake to discover that only a small quantity of silt has been deposited on the paved streets. They'll also find fabrics still intact. And, I have no doubt, they'll find the skeletons of men not long dead. Doubtless, this will amaze them.

They will write innumerable theses to explain that this water has a certain mysterious chemical component which makes it impossible for bones to decay. However, *mes amis,* the true explanation is very simple—entirely too simple to be grasped by the scientific mind.

They'll find that those men have been dead not longer than two years. And yet they are buried in a Roman city which flourished before Caesar. And the terrain on which this city is built is a blank spot on the map. It is on the northern slope of the High Atlas.

No topographer has ever carried his alidade that deep into northern Africa, and there are only a few of us who have known the Legion who can sketch the trails that are safe, the few water holes that exist in that bleached aridity.

We who have been in the Legion sometimes know more than the trails. Working for a pittance a day we should have known nothing of vast riches—gold piled in heaping stacks, glittering gems which might have graced the head of Cleopatra. No, there is entirely too much contrast there. We should never have known.

I sat behind a machine gun, bowing my head under a merciless sun which was sending heat waves writhing all up and down the sides of the bare brown mountains. The heat waves made a target jump like a 1912 movie. But if they were bad for me, so were they bad for the Berbers who lurked down in the ravine, or on the opposing slope—gray white swirls of burnoose, gone before a man could get a decent aim.

My only protection against the shrill whine of snipers' bullets was the rough-hewn *murette*—the rock wall we had built on our arrival. The machine-gun's black snout was thrust through an embrasure so as to command the slope which went down from us to the ravine bottom. Near at hand Chauchats were stacked—three of them, clean and ready. Back of me, in the poorly constructed pup tents, the remainder of my squad stretched out under canvas, panting in the heat, hoping for the coolness of night.

I had not shaved or washed for three weeks. One cannot keep clean on a swallow of water a day. Nor can one do a great deal to fight off thirst. The only water hole for miles was with us, inside the *murette,* and the man who named it a water hole was the century's greatest jester. It had been going dry, inch by inch, until now there remained but a damp scum over the bottom—green scum at that.

Within forty-eight hours our water would be gone, and the only answer to that predicament would be a pell-mell rush down the ravine toward the main command which lay some leagues to the east. It was doubtful whether we could get through those white robes; moreover, the district had been reported subdued. No patrols would be out checking on us. I had not sighted a plane for three days.

A man in the tent nearest me moaned incessantly. A sniper's bullet had caught him just under the belt, smashing his hip. He had been delirious for twelve hours. Soon he would die.

The five other men were silent save for their heavy breathing. Hungry and thirsty, baked by sun and caked with dirt, not yet rested after a long campaign, they found no heart to talk.

Although my eyes were burning with the shimmering haze of heat, I saw the movements across the ravine. Several Berbers sprang out from behind a rock the size of a moving van and began jumping up and down, waving their guns.

Suddenly a stone rolled down below. I boosted myself up to my knees and stared into the ravine. Not ten feet away from me a pair of beady black eyes set in a chisel-sharp face returned my stare.

The fellow had a knife clutched in his fist, a rifle across his back. Behind him came five others.

I grabbed the machine gun and depressed the muzzle as far as I could. The second man in the attacking party drew a revolver and fired. My cap went spinning away to thump against the tents. Hands were over the edge. I snapped down on the trips.

The first dozen shots caught the leader square in the face, hammering it into a raw mass of blood. The second burst cut the man with the revolver just above the belt line—cut him almost in two. Before the others could turn and run for it I centered my sights on them and let drive.

Their bodies went bumping and sliding down the slope. I helped them along with a few shots. In a moment there were six bundles of rags far below, lying motionless, gray white robes turning scarlet with blood.

Montrey, a small Frenchman and second in command,

came racing out of the first pup tent on all fours. He crawled over to me.

"Name of a name!" swore Montrey. "They are gone?"

"Yes," I told him.

"Confound it! I missed the fun."

"Wasn't any fun to it," I said. "If they'd come five feet further before I saw them they'd have gotten me. And they'd have gotten the rest of you before you could have reached your Lebels."

"Maybe," replied Montrey, seating himself and fumbling for a smoke.

"How is the little fellow?" I asked, referring to the wounded man.

"Copain? He's all right. Or will be in another three or four hours. He's lucky, that one. No more worry about water, no more worry about these Berber pigs."

"I think I'll go in and see him," I said.

Copain's eyes were wide open, but he did not see us. He was sprawled on his blankets. Flies, attracted by the blood, were already gathering. Copain was small and wiry. His yellow face was quite calm.

"How are you feeling?" I asked him. I knew that he would not answer, that he had not heard, but I felt that I should say something.

But Copain surprised us. His lips drew open and he twisted his shoulders around. By the light of his eyes I knew that he was deep in delirium.

"You'll get it all now, won't you, Tanner? All of it!" Copain's glassy eyes flickered. "You're a swine, Tanner."

Montrey looked at me quickly. This Tanner that Copain talked about had been killed some weeks before in a line skirmish far to the east. And Copain had been there at the man's finish.

"But before I see you get all of it, I'll take this gun—this gun, see? The gun that killed André! I'll take this gun and shoot you down like a pig! You won't get it if I'm not there. We've waited too long."

Montrey tried to smooth Copain's forehead.

"Easy, soldier."

But Copain threshed out his arms and with amazing strength threw Montrey back from him.

"Get away from me! Get away from me! You can't talk me out of it. You can't do me out of my share! I'll get it in spite of you and hell and the Berbers. And I'll spend it on cars and women!" He was shouting now, his glazed eyes narrowed.

"Quiet," I said. "It's Montrey and your corporal. It's all right, Copain."

The flap of the pup tent lifted and curious, unshaven faces peered in.

Montrey shook his head.

"He won't live an hour if we let him roll around like that."

"Which makes it three hours less he'll have to suffer if he comes out of this," I said. "I wonder what the devil he's talking about."

Copain, through that fog of delirium, must have heard me.

"You know what I'm talking about, Tanner. It was you that went with me when we discovered it. It was you that said to wait a while until we could get André out of the deal before we made a break."

"André?" muttered a man in the entrance. "He was found shot in the back last month—shot with a Lebel."

"Sure he was!" howled Copain. "Sure he was! I did it, didn't I, Tanner. I did it. He wanted all of it. Every last bit of it. And so I shot him."

I didn't like to crouch there listening to another man's secrets. I started to back out but the crowd in the door wouldn't let me through.

Copain was talking again.

"You couldn't even find your way back there! You weren't ever in the Intelligence, Tanner. You need me and you'll take me with you!"

I didn't like the sudden light which came into Montrey's eyes.

"I'll take you with me, Copain," he said. "Just you and I, eh? We'll go get all of it. And because you know the way and have the map, I'll let you have sixty percent."

At first I thought that Montrey was just trying to humor Copain. I should have known better than that. I should have been on my guard. God knows, if I had been, maybe some of those men would be living today.

Copain appeared to be easier.

"All right, Tanner. Just you and I. And I get sixty percent because of that map. You don't know where it is, but I do, and I'll find it as soon as I'm off this post. We'll make a run for it tonight. There's plenty of it for both of us in that town, isn't there, Tanner?

"More than fifty Moor barbs could carry. Jewels, Tanner —think of it. And gold. I'll take the jewels. Gold is too heavy, Tanner. And I'm . . . I'm . . . tired. . . ."

Copain sagged back on his blankets. His eyes flickered shut. Phlegm rattled in his throat. His fingers contracted like claws.

I moved forward again and drew the blanket over Copain's face. Then I crawled backward out of the tent and went over to the *murette*. I sat down on a rock, facing the opposite side of the ravine.

Suddenly, Ivan's machine gun jerked out of the embrasure and pointed at me. Another gun rammed its blunt muzzle against the small of my back. I looked up and saw Montrey's queerly tight face.

CHAPTER TWO

Mutiny

I gave my kepi a tug and looked at Ivan. "Perhaps, Ivan, you had better save those bullets for the Berbers and point that machine gun back into the ravine."

Ivan's dark, sunken eyes did not waver from my face. Nor did the machine gun.

Montrey smiled.

"Mon corporal," he said, "I have said a few words to the men. They have decided to give you a chance."

"Very nice of them, *mon général,*" I snapped.

"You might do better," replied Montrey, "by sitting there and answering a few questions." He jerked his gun at Ivan and his smile broadened. *"Mon corporal,* why did you join the Legion?"

"What are you driving at, Montrey?"

He struck a pose, looking like a scarecrow, and I would have laughed at him had it not been for the revolver and machine gun.

"We want to know if you wish to continue serving France."

"Yes," I replied, as quietly as I could. "If you're talking about desertion, we don't know anything about the country to the northwest of us and I don't think we could even get through east to the main command. These devils think too much of our Lebel rifles and they hate the *Makhzan* on general principles. We'll have to stick until we get a relief column."

"Mon corporal," *he said, "I have said a few words to the men.
They have decided to give you a chance."*

"Relief column, *hein*? You think they care enough about a squad to send a relief column after it—running the risk of losing a whole company in doing so? You are *cafard, mon corporal*. You think only in terms of brass bands and medals. If you do not wish to come with us, then we will find this map and go ourselves." He lifted the revolver. "Without you."

"So that's the way the wind blows. You'll murder me and light out yourselves. How do you think you will find your way? No one has ever marked these peaks. You have no charts. You would be lost a day's march away from this base."

"You have a compass," smiled Montrey. "We would like to borrow that."

I reached into the right breast pocket of my tunic and pulled out the compass. It was primarily designed for determining azimuths and interceptions for machine-gun fire. It had a raised wire sight and when one looked through the glass eyepiece he saw a number on the compass disc and the object which would determine a bearing.

I handed it to Montrey and with a glance to make certain that Ivan Njivi was still covering me, Montrey raised himself up until he could see over the parapet. He took a sight on a red boulder across the gap.

"It is in good order," said Montrey. "I thank you. Now we have no further need of you. Understand, *mon corporal*, that we shoot you not because we do not like you but because it is irksome to be hampered by a higher rank in our midst. Ivan! You might as well finish him." Montrey stepped quickly away and Ivan squinted at me through the sights.

I managed a smile.

"Wait a minute, Montrey. Before you are so foolish as to kill me, take another sight at right angles to the one you just took."

He eyed me for several seconds. Then, feeling that I was doing more than stalling for time, he raised himself and sighted another boulder. He sank back in a moment, his face blank.

"Why—why, *mon Dieu!* This reads almost the same! It must be broken!"

"No," I said. "It is not broken. Perhaps you have heard that iron deflects a compass needle. It so happens that these mountains are so full of iron ore that it is impossible to obtain a correct compass reading. You might as well throw that instrument away, Montrey."

"But," cried Montrey, "how can you find your way around?"

I was breathing easier.

"Montrey, I don't think you ever heard of trigonometry. Nor calculus. Nor could you name a single constellation in the sky."

His face was still blank.

"What is a constellation?"

"A body of stars," I replied. "I was once a civil engineer, Montrey. They have to know such things. That is why I was on Intelligence work the first few months I was in the Legion. Not spy Intelligence, but mapping service. Because I mapped better than the officer in charge of the party, he became afraid that I would use my knowledge against him. He had me transferred to the line companies. Did you hear what Copain said before he died? Copain was an Intelligence man, also versed in mapping."

Montrey gestured to Ivan and scuttled back to Copain's tent. The three men dived in with Montrey. The canvas shook, fell apart. Angrily they threw back the khaki rags and spread all of poor Copain's meager belongings on the ground. With ruthless, lustful hands they set to work. Equipment was torn to shreds. Even the blanket was taken from the dead man and ripped apart.

These men, a few moments before, had been good soldiers, but now, with the scent of gold in their nostrils, they had gone mad. Too much privation, bad food, too little water. It was an old story, that madness.

In a few moments they discovered that Copain's kepi had a double lining. They slit the innermost one and then Montrey was standing there holding a piece of mapping paper in shaking hands. Three unshaven faces peered over his shoulders. Ivan wanted to go but he did not leave the gun.

Presently, Montrey came over to me and threw the paper in my lap. "Intelligence, *hein*? I see but little intelligence to that, *mon corporal*."

The sheet was covered with accurately drawn lines and minute figures. The readings were all in longitude and latitude, figured down to seconds. To a layman, it was an aimless jumble, but to a former Intelligence man, it was quite comprehensible. Vividly so.

Copain had taken vast pains with this map. He showed the High Atlas with wriggling, correctly read contours. He had spotted peaks, estimated their elevation; he had drawn a small square, marking it with the recognized symbol for stone walls—a series of circles. It was easy to see that this city lay in a valley between two mountain ranges.

Also that a river ran through the exact center of the town and found its way out of the valley by means of a deep gorge.

"There is much intelligence to this, but it will do none of you any good. Go back to your tents and get out of this sun. We'll have another attack tonight."

"No you don't!" snarled Montrey. "You are going to lead us to that place. And we are leaving at dusk."

"And what if I refuse?"

Montrey glanced about him. A coil of line was at one end of the *murette*. I knew then what he intended to do. A band around the forehead, drawn tight as a tourniquet, is a pain no man can stand.

I decided that I could only get out of this by smashing my way through. While his eyes were still on the rope I suddenly grabbed Montrey's wrist.

With a howl he jumped away, trying to bring up the seized gun. Ivan crouched lower over the machine gun, unwilling to shoot Montrey.

Montrey twisted about, threw me off balance and jumped back. Ivan's eye was tight against the machine-gun sight. He pressed the trips.

It was Ivan's pride that he was the best machine gunner in the Legion. I knew that his slugs would hammer me to pulp in an instant.

Suddenly Ivan ceased to fire. I looked up, expecting to find myself dead. But Ivan sat beside the gun, grinning foolishly and staring at the sights. He looked at Montrey and shrugged, pointing to the sights.

Montrey, half-crouched, eyed the revolver which lay in the dust halfway between us.

"I'm sorry," said Ivan, chuckling. "It's the sights. They were set for six hundred yards. I fired over the top of his head."

Like a huge ape, he rocked back and forth. His mind was too flighty, too childish, to see any further than the joke. He, Ivan, the best machine gunner in the Legion, had failed to notice that his sights were set for six hundred yards when he was firing at thirty feet.

Montrey relaxed and looked once more at the rope.

I sighed.

"Oh, what the deuce, Montrey. We can't stay here. Let's try for Casablanca way to the northwest. If we happen across the pipe dream of Copain's, we'll take along the loot. But I'll go on one condition."

"Condition?"

"Yes. That I am still in command of my own squad and that my word is law. We go as a body of *Legionnaires,* not as a rabble. Remember, Montrey, I am the only one that can take you to that place."

Montrey relaxed and shrugged.

"All right, *mon corporal.*"

CHAPTER THREE

Berber Bullets

I assembled my men after they had finished the task of burying Copain. They looked at me with feverish eyes. Montrey licked his thirst-swollen lips. Ivan Njivi fumbled with his hands. Kraus, the German, Gian, the Italian, and Maurice, another Frenchman, made up the remainder of the squad. We had buried the other two a few days before.

"Listen closely," I said. "After moonrise it will be too late to get away, but I suspect that the Berbers will be waiting until they have light enough to make their attack. That should come within the next hour.

"We will file along this ridge, one at a time. Then we will drop down into a ravine. That point will be our rendezvous. From there I will have to lead the way because we know nothing of what lies beyond."

They nodded, nervously. I knew that they did not fear the Berbers we might meet. They were overcome by the thought that they might have enough money at the end of this trek to live the rest of their lives in luxury. I knew that they would be hard to handle—harder even than when drunk.

There is nothing quite as bad as gold madness.

I divided the Chauchats and ammunition among them. When they had finished their *paquetage*, Montrey spoke up.

"I suppose, *mon corporal*, that because of your rank, you

do not find it necessary to carry a load other than your own equipment."

"Pardon, *m'sieu,*" I bowed, "but you have forgotten the dynamite and gunpowder that was left here with us. It makes a heavier load than any of you are carrying."

"And what do you want with that?"

"If only to keep it from falling into Berber hands, I take it along." With that, I dug the explosives out of the hole in the cliff face and packaged them. They had been used in constructing this post and when the company had left us there, their Moorish barbs had been too overloaded to carry them.

I led off a few minutes before the moon came up. The ridge was like a knife back, hard to walk along. An incautious step would send a warning shower of boulders down into the ravine.

A hundred yards away from the post I stopped and listened. I could hear rocks rolling down in the gully. That meant that our friends the Berbers were on the move. A shadowy figure was close behind me. That would be Ivan, judging from his hulk.

As I reached the end of the ridge, I started the vertical descent to the bottom. To fight in the High Atlas, a soldier has to be half mountain goat, half pack barb, half Alpineer, and half crystal gazer. That makes two soldiers, doesn't it? Well, no matter. You have to be at least three to stay in the Legion.

Ivan dropped down beside me and slid into the shadow of the moon. He was uncannily silent for so huge a man. Then came the stolid Kraus. After him were Gian, Maurice and finally Montrey.

Montrey's whisper was shrill.

"They're starting to attack the post! We'd better get out of here. When they find we're gone they'll be able to track us. Those jackals have the noses of hounds."

"All right. Maurice, you're rear guard. See that they don't jump us and don't waste too many of those Chauchat bullets, get me?"

Maurice had a ratlike face. I didn't like his tone when he said, *"Oui, mon commandant!"*

I turned to Gian.

"You keep bullets in your gun, understand? I'm leading off with Montrey."

Gian stroked the Chauchat's butt.

"Do not lead off too far, *mon commandant*. My range is better than a thousand yards—and in this moonlight—" he broke off with an oily smile.

I knew that it was no use to try the mailed fist with them. They were all half-crazed.

We had just started off when all hell broke loose back at the post. The Berbers had reached it and judging from the sounds they were tearing it apart.

Stepping off as fast as we could, we heard Maurice go into action. Looking back I saw the top of the ridge thick with white, clearly shown by the moon. When the Chauchat rattled into full swing, men began to drop. They came down like shot gulls. Then I heard a roar of angry voices.

Men poured out at us from the ravine below the post.

Maurice stopped firing and came up to us on the run. We reached a bend in the gulch and turned it. Another bend presented itself dead ahead. We made that one. I snatched Maurice's Chauchat.

"Go on!" I bellowed. "Make the next bend and cover my retreat with the machine gun!"

But Montrey in turn took the Chauchat from me and thrust it back at Maurice.

"No! You've got to lead us to that town! Maurice, you heard his orders. Get busy!"

Almost at once the Chauchat began to rave. The swirl of burnoose and the glint of moonlight on white headcloths was momentarily checked. The hillmen dived into cover behind boulders and their dead splotched the ravine floor with motionless white patches.

We made the next bend and I halted. Montrey jerked at my arm.

"Come on, you fool!" he cried.

"We've got to cover Maurice's retreat!" I bellowed.

"To the devil with Maurice!"

I struck him on the mouth. Gian had hesitated for an instant and I pointed down the gully. Gian leveled his auto-rifle over the top of a boulder and let drive. Maurice, head held low, sprinted across the patches of moonlight and came up to us, swearing and panting.

"You'll cover the next!" I snapped at Montrey.

His face went gray, but he took Gian's position behind the gun. I knew that Montrey would not reverse the piece on us.

He was far too busy stemming the tide of white which rose like a wave before him.

Maurice seemed to understand. He choked out, *"Merci,"* as we ran on.

Ivan had stopped. He had slung the machine gun to its tripod behind a rock. I looked ahead to see that another white blur had materialized to our front. We were hemmed in front and rear. A boulder crashed near at hand. On the left cliff side I saw a flurry of cloth. The Berbers were up there, trying to smash us with rocks.

There was only one answer to that. We had to scale a sheer wall in full pack and in full view of those very competent riflemen, the Berbers.

Ivan started to fire short, snapping bursts. Men sought cover from the leaden sleet. Gian had covered Montrey's retreat with an indifferent fire and Montrey was with us again. I pointed to the high summit above us.

"Who has the rope?" And when it was forthcoming, I slid out of my pack and gripped for the first handholds. "Get those devils on the other side up there. And when I drop this end to you, pass up the machine gun on it. Then send Gian with his Chauchat. I think we can make it."

Climbing, I wondered how long our ammunition would last at this rate. Chauchats and machine guns have a way of using up lead and powder. On the cliff face I was aware that I made a tempting target, but I had not dared to trust any of the others. Not that they were yellow. You can't stay in the Legion and be yellow. But they were off balance, giddy.

A slug showered me with sharp fragments. Another

73

twitched at my kepi, but by some miracle it stayed on. I remember thinking that I would rather lose my life than my kepi. Without that headgear, I would have lost my mind under the onslaught of sun.

The top seemed very far away, though it was less than three hundred feet. I stopped midway and sent down the line for the machine gun. Bracing myself I pulled it up.

As I fed in a new belt I shouted for Gian and went to work driving the surrounding hillmen away from the sniping points. In something like three minutes, Gian was there with me. I put him behind the machine gun and went on up.

The second half of the trip was more difficult than the first, but with the machine gun at that elevation, the sniping had almost ceased. With a thankful grunt I wrapped my fingers over the edge of the cliff and hoisted myself up.

A movement over my head caught my eye. I was staring straight into black, contracted eyes. The man's knife was reaching out playfully to sink itself into my ribs.

CHAPTER FOUR

The Skeleton

THE short scrap of that afternoon flashed across my mind. Then it had been the Berber who had been below, trying to reach up to the *murette,* and whom I had pounded into a bloody and battered pulp with bullets. It appeared that the tables were turned. I did not seem to fear the awful pain of the knife thrust half so much as the fall. Three hundred feet is a long way down. The white kepis below me looked like dimes.

To do it I had to let go with both hands. I jerked down a foot, dangling over space. Then I had the hillman's knife wrist in my hand. He tried to shake me without pulling back. He was wise, that one. He knew what I intended to do.

He must have felt himself slipping too close to the edge. Pebbles were showering down all around me. He jerked back and suddenly I was on hard earth. I rolled over, taking him with me. Behind him burnooses swirled. I would have to act fast.

Planting both my feet in his belly, I shoved up and back. He catapulted headfirst over the edge, screaming, through emptiness.

A rifle spat beside my face. I snatched the barrel and twisted it away. Evidently, the hillmen were too terrified at their

*Then I had the hillman's knife wrist in my hand. He tried to
shake me without pulling back. He was wise, that one.
He knew what I intended to do.*

GET 4 FREE BOOKS!

You can have the titles in the Stories from the Golden Age delivered to your door by signing up for the book club. Start today, and we'll send you **4 FREE BOOKS** (worth $39.80) as your reward.

The collection includes 80 volumes (book or audio) by master storyteller L. Ron Hubbard in the genres of science fiction, fantasy, mystery, adventure and western, originally penned for the pulp magazines of the 1930s and '40s.

YES! ☐

Sign me up for the Stories from the Golden Age Book Club and send me my first book for $9.95 with my **4 FREE BOOKS** (FREE shipping). I will pay only $9.95 each month for the subsequent titles in the series. Shipping is FREE and I can cancel any time I want to.

First Name _____ Middle Name _____ Last Name _____

Address _____

City _____ State _____ ZIP _____

Telephone _____ E-mail _____

Credit/Debit Card #: _____

Card ID# (last 3 or 4 digits): _____ Exp Date: _____ / _____

Date (month/day/year) _____ / _____ / _____

Signature: _____

Comments: _____

Check here ☑ to receive a FREE Stories from the Golden Age catalog or go to: **GoldenAgeStories.com**.

Thank you!

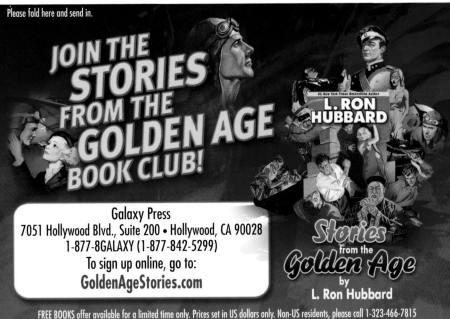

companion's fate. They turned and ran. It was an easy matter to cut them down. Their white burnooses made excellent targets.

Once more I lowered the rope which I had coiled about my waist. Presently Gian and the machine gun were both there. And, after another short interval, Maurice and Montrey were on top and out of sight behind a boulder. Kraus, grunting and sweating, rolled over the edge and reached back to help Ivan.

I took a sight along the ridge, discovering that it ran in the direction we wanted to travel. There did not seem to be any immediate end to it and so we struck out, running rapidly from cover to cover, keeping the Berbers out of sight with a swift and certain rear-guard action, taking turns at staying behind.

By the moonlight, about 2 AM, I stopped and consulted Copain's map. He had marked a water hole about a mile from our course.

"We'll get something to drink now," I said. "But we may have to fight for it."

"Why so?" challenged Montrey. "Our retreat is losing those devils at the rate of a hundred a mile."

"There are other tribes through here," I replied. "And water holes are few and far between. See that fire about six miles behind us?"

He looked back and stared at the blinking point of light.

"They're passing a blanket before that flame," I said. "They must have learned a few tricks from the French. Anybody ahead of us will be on the scout, looking for us. And they're bound to protect the water holes."

"Oui, mon commandant," said Montrey with an ugly, twisted smile. "You frighten me out of my senses."

Ivan laughed, but Maurice fumbled with his Chauchat as though he wanted to squirt lead.

We went on. The dryness of our throats was increased by the rising dust. But the others did not seem to care. Their minds were far ahead of us, over the ranges of the High Atlas, and they dreamed of a mysterious, uncharted city where riches could be picked up for the effort of reaching.

We spotted the water hole far below us and began the descent to it, sliding through loose stone. In the lead, I stopped and held up my hand. The others stopped behind me. An errant breeze had come up from the ravine and with it had come the odor of wet steam. The message was obvious. A fire had burned there until a few moments before. The Berbers had poured water over it in the hopes of ambushing us when we came down to drink.

"They're waiting for us," I said.

"Let's go down," insisted Montrey. "We can't go without water forever."

"All right, Montrey. If you're so thirsty, lead the way with an auto-rifle."

He went ahead after giving me a hard look. Ivan had been busy with his pet. Mounting a rock, he straddled the tripod legs and pulled back the loading handle of the machine gun. I followed Montrey.

A rifle roared ten feet in front. Other rifles began to rave. The Chauchats went into action; the machine gun rolled out a guttural bass to the overture. Berbers howled. That which had been a black rocky pit suddenly swirled with white robes and lashing flame.

I dived behind a rock and began to fire into the thick of it with my Lebel. It was impossible to miss.

Hastily organizing themselves, the hillmen rolled out of the semicircular rock amphitheatre like a typhoon. In an instant they were all around me. Ivan's gun sent a burst ricocheting off my boulder. The Berbers drew away from me.

I saw Kraus pick up a hillman by the waist and pitch him bodily back into the thick of the rush.

With three Chauchats and a machine gun backing up rifle fire, the noise was head-splitting. A hundred men pounding on a hundred anvils could not have made a greater racket. Evidently it was too much for the Berbers, for to my right the gorge began to fill up with men.

For a heart-stopping instant I thought that reinforcements had come for the hillmen. Then a shaft of moonlight showed me that their faces were turned away. I sent a parting clip into the stragglers and then silence settled down upon the water hole.

As I approached the small pool, I saw a big hillman lying in my path. He was not dead, though the lower part of his burnoose was covered with blood. Suddenly he rolled over and grabbed for his rifle. As the muzzle came up, my rifle drilled a hole between his eyes.

We wasted but little time in filling our canteens and our mouths with water. Though it was muddy and foul it tasted like nectar. The hillmen had left a few kettles of boiled mutton on the scene. It was still warm and we ate it, scooping the greasy mess out with our bare hands.

Ten minutes later we were once more on the trail, heading northwest toward the square on Copain's map. Kraus was limping and saying nothing about it. He was afraid that we would leave him if he confessed a wound. I let him be. His first-aid packet was open and I knew he had dressed the hole. Maurice's jaw was covered with blood from a torn ear.

By a combination of luck and skill I found that we were on the trail which had been marked down by Copain. Dawn broke to find us toiling up the side of a mountain range, heading toward a pass. We had marched hard and fast as Legionnaires are supposed to march and now we would need protection from the sun and daylight attacks.

We gained the summit. It was Montrey that spotted an old *murette* halfway up a cliff. We made for it. I was rather puzzled by its presence as this country had never been posted. However, Copain and Tanner and André had come this way and this must have been their handiwork.

Maurice was the first one over the wall. He dropped out of sight and then came back to give the others a hand. A slanting ray of sunlight struck us, showing up the old camp in detail. I stopped halfway over and stared at the base of the cliff across the compound.

A skeleton lay there in the storm-beaten clothes of a

Legionnaire. His tattered kepi had rolled several feet away. His boots were cracked by sun and dust. His pack had been torn apart and lay scattered about him.

From the back of the faded tunic there protruded a French bayonet!

CHAPTER FIVE

Gold Madness

THE man's kit revealed his name—or the name he had borne in the Legion. It was Schrader, onetime Intelligence private. I had never known him very well, but I did know that he was one of the squad who had been with Copain on that mapping expedition.

Tanner, André, Copain and now Schrader. All these men were dead, two of them because they knew too much about a city lost in this mountain waste.

When I tried to pull the bayonet out of Schrader's back, it would not come. There was no flesh to hold it and I rolled the skeleton back from it.

The bayonet was embedded three inches in the ground. They had killed him while he slept!

I was not especially concerned that Copain and Tanner and André had killed Schrader. I was thinking about my own neck. When Montrey and the others got to the city they might think they had no further use for me. Perhaps they would strike out for the coast without me. Perhaps they had learned enough about the direction of these mountains to guide themselves.

That day I slept away from them with one hand on my gun, the other on my bayonet.

When the midday heat was gone, we buried the skeleton.

Montrey was smiling as though he possessed a new inspiration. I knew what that inspiration was. Montrey knew now that he did not have to divide with the rest. Montrey was thinking that he would get it all for himself.

Aside from a very occasional bullet from great range we were not much troubled by the hillmen. They had developed a healthy respect for the auto-rifle and machine gun.

With darkness shrouding our movements we hit the trail again. All that night we tramped over mountains, through passes, down ravines, and when dawn came again we had progressed twenty-seven miles.

We had to build our own *murette* that morning, but on the three succeeding days we found them built for us.

That mapping squad had taken no chances with the Berbers.

Six days' march from our original base, we made camp on a high summit which overlooked countless square miles of upended country.

Montrey sat on a boulder beside me.

"I suppose you know just exactly where you are, don't you. Right to a dot."

"Pretty near," I replied, disregarding his surly tone.

"Wouldn't care to point out the valley, would you?"

"No. I don't think I would."

"Afraid you'd get it in the neck?"

"I know I would, Montrey. Just as sure as I can see that valley from this point."

The statement brought the others to their feet. They crowded around me, their faces lit up, their eyes burning with greed.

"Show us!" cried Gian.

"You'll be there when the moon comes up late tonight," I assured him.

Posting two sentries, I rolled over against a boulder and went to sleep, facing the *murette* where Montrey and Maurice were standing the first watch.

I don't know how long I slept, but I woke up on my feet. The machine gun was going full blast, with Montrey behind the butt. Maurice was sprawled over the edge of the parapet, blood gushing from a spot between his eyes.

In an instant I was beside him, a Chauchat in my hands. Down the slope three men were scurrying away, their white robes ballooning away from them. Montrey got two with one burst.

I shot the other.

"How did they get so close to you?" I demanded, staring at Maurice.

Montrey shrugged and smiled crookedly.

"They got close to you once, didn't they?"

Pulling Maurice back into the compound, I inspected the wound. Looking up, I said, "Close is right, Montrey. There are powder marks around this hole."

Before he could jump away I wrenched his revolver out of his belt and sniffed at the barrel.

It had certainly been fired within ten minutes.

All the others were up. Kraus glowered at Montrey. Gian licked his lips. Ivan stood with widespread feet, glaring.

"Listen," I said. "Watch Montrey. He just shot Maurice under the cover of that attack and he may try to get the rest of you."

Ivan, slower witted than the rest, growled, "Well, what is wrong with that? Maurice was playing in with you, *mon corporal*. It was—"

"Shut up, pig!" snapped Montrey.

I studied their faces for the space of a minute. I saw then that they were not glaring at Montrey. Their eyes were on me. I already could feel the sharp points of their needle bayonets going through my flesh.

I did not sleep any more that day.

CHAPTER SIX

Fight in the Mosque

IN the white moonlight we approached the walls of the city—or what had once been a city. Tier after tier of stones had been standing there for hundreds of years. I am not enough of an archaeologist to give you the exact description and type and period, but even to my unpracticed eyes, this seemed the work of Romans.

Approaching a wall which had dwarfed us, the others turned to me. Montrey smiled, his dark eyes were blazing.

"You think we cannot find our way out of here?" he said.

"I don't know, Montrey," I replied. "It would be rather difficult without a compass. Of course, it's nothing to me if you want to get lost in these mountains. Nothing at all."

Then Montrey pointed to something which I had not seen before. It was a stone-paved road leading out to the northwest. A Roman road, built nine feet into the ground, imperishable. It would show the way.

They would not need me anymore.

Simultaneously with that discovery, Gian made another.

"The Berbers!" he cried. "They didn't follow us down here!"

All eyes swept to the southeast toward the empty mountains. It was true.

They had not followed. But it was not a cause for relief. There must be something in this city which they feared.

I stepped away from the others. By moonlight it was impossible to see very far with any distinctness, even though the moon was as bright as an arc lamp.

Looking back at the town I saw the gates. Something was moving beside them. Something white. Had the Berbers followed us after all? I did not think so. The hillmen would want nothing better than an open plain to start an attack. As we were without cover they could wipe us out by the very crush of numbers.

Montrey trotted toward the gate and I went up to him. The white thing had disappeared. Montrey tested the tall iron grilling. In this high altitude, the iron did not show any great signs of wear or rust—a fact which is very usual but which caused me a bad moment. The grill was shiny at the height of a man's hand!

"We'd better get out of here," I said. "If we don't, I'm afraid there won't be any of us left to go back."

"You should worry about going back," snapped Montrey. He swung around and I saw that he held a Chauchat at waist level. By the moonlight I could see the fire in his eyes.

I dived to the right, expecting the impact of bullets at any instant. But instead I heard a creak of rusty hinges. I looked back at Montrey and past him I beheld a white robe. The gates were open!

The man said something in a language which sounded like Arabic, but before the sentence was finished, Montrey had wheeled on him with the auto-rifle. Almost in the same instant, a sword flashed in the gatekeeper's hand.

Montrey let drive. The powder flame turned the wall a dull red. It seemed that the gun went on forever before the gatekeeper collapsed.

Kraus, Gian and Ivan came on the run, faces set, guns ready. They headed straight for the gate.

"Don't go in!" I shouted. "The town is occupied!"

But I might as well have told the silent hills to move. Montrey in the lead, they swept in through the portals and ran down a narrow street, boots ringing against the stone, their bandoliers clanking. I rammed after them, pack jarring my back.

Instantly the town was alive with men. They spewed from every doorway. Crude lanterns jumped into being. A concerted howl went up from a thousand throats.

The four ahead of me would not stop to make a stand. They were mad with the lust for gold. They did not seem to realize that there would be no escape for them, ringed as they were with walls and men.

Ahead was a cleared space—probably the old forum. The stones were worn and in the moonlight the white pillars of the buildings which faced it loomed like so many ghostly soldiers.

On a rise a hundred feet away stood a square, squat building built like the Acropolis. Montrey headed for it.

To the rear of the three others ran Gian. His head was lowered and his teeth were set. From a roof above us a rifle cracked with a streak of red flame. Gian stumbled and caved in.

I paused long enough to snatch up the auto-rifle and the

cartridge belts. Another rifle spat down at me and knocked my kepi away. My auto-rifle barked and the gun above me clattered to the street, followed by a white-robed figure.

Recovering the kepi, I sprinted on. A small bridge was underfoot and I could hear the gurgling wash of the river beneath.

Montrey knew what he was doing when he headed for the square building above. It was the only one which could be defended—and it was obviously an old Roman temple.

I toiled up the steps. Above I saw Montrey unlimber an auto-rifle. Ivan was already at work. The machine gun rapped and roared, sending screaming bullets into the streets below.

I made the entrance of the building with one last jump and dived inside, heading for the rear.

Two statues were in this dim interior, statues of the Roman gods. But they were lying on their sides, broken into great fragments. Mohammedanism had come to this city, that was plain. Therefore, this was a mosque.

A shadowy body was catapulted at me, knife shimmering in a tense hand. I sidestepped and pulled the trigger. The man went skittering back, flat on the floor, driven there by my bullets.

I was not a moment too soon in reaching the rear of the mosque. Men came swarming up the hillside, weapons gleaming beneath the white moon.

Bracing the Chauchat against a pillar, I let them have it. The line wavered. Those in the rear were knocked back by those who fell in front.

No cover was available on that hillside. After the first rush was checked, even while the leaders exhorted their men to go on, I started at the left side and fired in an arc to the right. Pausing midway I fed more bullets into the smoking breech. The arc went on through.

In less than a minute the hillside was carpeted with white—nothing stirred.

Before I could get my breath I saw that I had not deterred the remaining forces in the least. They were forming at the bottom once again, ready for a second charge.

Although the Chauchat was hot enough to melt, I hammered three short bursts into the group across the forum just to show them that they were far from out of range.

I reached back confidently to where I had dropped the bandoliers. I reached further back, fumbling with the collapsed canvas. Suddenly it occurred to me that I was all out of ammunition.

I sprinted for the front of the mosque, risking an attack on the rear in my absence. The machine gun had gone silent as had the other auto-rifles.

Ivan was sprawled across his weapon, hands still on the trip. A pool of blood was widening on the white stone.

I whirled about and stared down the platform. Gian was doubled up, moaning, hitching himself toward me.

Gian's face was twisted in agony. He pressed pain-stiffened hands against his belly. Through the reddened fingers I saw that his belt had been shot away.

From within the mosque I heard Montrey's voice laughing

shrilly. Then I heard Kraus' bellow of rage. Gian was close
to me now, his eyes pleading. I knew what he wanted.

I unstrapped Ivan's rifle, jacked a bullet into the chamber
and sent it sliding toward Gian. I turned my back and went
into the mosque. The crack of the Lebel outside was dull,
muffled.

Montrey's laugh was there again and I ran toward it. I saw
an oil lamp, fed by mutton fat, hanging from the wall. Below
it, bending over a chest, stood Montrey and Kraus. Some
bright-colored stones were still rolling on the floor. Montrey
had jerked a necklace away from Kraus.

They straightened up and I knew they had not heard me
enter. Kraus reached back for his rifle, his face scarlet with
anger. Montrey's revolver was there first. The revolver barked.

Kraus jerked himself erect, rising on his toes. Montrey
fired again and Kraus fell face forward to the stone.

My own rifle was off my back. The revolver went spinning
away from Montrey's suddenly red hand as I shot from the
waist.

His face was blank with surprise. He recovered instantly.
"Curse you!"

"Shut up. The rest are dead," I snapped. "We've got to
get out of here and get out fast. I'm all out of bullets for this
auto-rifle and there aren't ten shots left in that machine gun.
We can't hold out, understand? It's going to take the two of
us to get out of here!"

With that I went over to the man I killed in the mosque. I
stripped him of his white robe and found it filthy with grease.
Bringing it back, I laid it out flat before the chest.

Montrey, unarmed and realizing what I had said was true, dipped his hands into the chest and began to scoop out handfuls of stuff which glittered and shimmered in the light of the swinging oil lamp. Several bright bars lay in the chest but I shook my head.

"No gold, get me? It's too heavy. And to blazes with that amber you've got!"

Grudgingly, Montrey let the amber slide back and scooped out another double handful of gems. Wrapping the ends of the robe around the glittering heap, I emptied my pack of everything that I did not think I could use. But that did not include the many pounds of gunpowder and dynamite that I had hauled all these torturous miles. Montrey looked on, sullenly.

"How are we going to get out?" he muttered. His wounded hand had sobered him.

"Follow me," I ordered.

From the rear of the mosque came a medley of yells. They had discovered that I was not at the top of those steps, and they were coming up.

Montrey and I stopped by the front pillars. I hurriedly gathered up the rifles. I extracted the bolt from the machine gun and then demolished the working parts with a smash against the stone.

Ivan's dead eyes seemed to follow us as we plunged down the steps toward the bridge.

Gian no longer had eyes. A Lebel bullet fired by his own hand had finished him.

But we had no time to worry about dead men. Very live

men rose up before us like *ifrīts*. Guns started up. Slugs whined about us like angry wasps.

Heads down, burdened by excess rifles, we ran toward the bridge.

The River of Death

WE made the bridge because we ran too fast and changed our course too often to make good targets.

I dropped the rifles to the deck of the nearest barge and then followed them over the edge. Montrey landed behind me like a cat.

Casting off the rough hempen line, we shoved the scow out into the swift stream which bisected the town. That done, I snatched up an auto-rifle and fed the last clip into the breech.

The men who had assembled on the bridge over our heads hastily drew back under the hail of bullets. The snipers along the river banks shrieked and dived for shelter. The stream carried us swiftly toward the aperture which let the river flow on through the valley to the steep gorge at the far end.

Then I heard the clatter of horses' hoofs far away. Mounting their barbs, Allah's children were making certain that they would reach the gorge before we did. I wondered why we should not be able to slip on through the gorge. I found out soon enough.

Montrey, thinking that the danger was passed, turned on me. "I suppose you think I'm going to let you—"

I lowered my rifle.

"You're staying with me, Montrey, until I don't need you any longer."

"Got an idea that you can take me into Legion headquarters or something like that?"

"Shut up and lay on with that pole. We've got to get to the gorge before those horsemen. Otherwise, we're liable to be out of luck."

That brought him back to momentary truce. He snatched up the pole and plied it with a will. The arch in the west wall of the town passed swiftly over our heads. When we were out on the plain, floating swiftly along, the horsemen rounded the near wall and thundered along the bank toward us.

I leveled the auto-rifle and fired three bursts, emptying several saddles. I discovered once and for all, as I started to fire again, that the auto-rifles were useless. We were out of everything but rifle bullets.

Without ceremony I dumped the three Chauchats into the river and followed them up with all the Lebels but two. At least they would never fall into Berber hands.

The plain whisked by. Ahead I heard the mutter of falling water. I knew then why they seemed so certain of catching up with us. That gorge was filled with rapids, perhaps falls, as are most river gorges. I knew that we didn't have a chance. No more rapid-firing guns—only two Lebels and a questionable supply of ammunition for those. The auto-rifles and the machine gun were what had kept us from annihilation thus far.

Just before we reached the gorge, I headed the scow into the bank. We jumped out and let the barge float on.

Running again, I saw a footpath that seemed to travel along the riverside.

Montrey slacked up.

"What's the use?" he cried. "We haven't anything with which to defend ourselves. They'll hunt us down no matter how far away we travel!"

I did not answer him. I was too busy working in the cliff side. From a short distance away came the pounding of hoofs, as ominous as distant artillery fire. Montrey stood looking back, gripping his Lebel with white-knuckled hands.

I had drilled a dozen deep holes in the soft, crumbly rock, so I unstrapped my pack and hauled out the dynamite and gunpowder. It was a moment's work to cap the sticks and apply the fuse.

Stuffing the holes full of explosive, hoping that this would give us a temporary respite, I applied a match. The fuse sputtered.

The hoofs were nearer now, less than two hundred yards away. Montrey saw what I had done. He ran ahead of me. The horses were almost to the gap.

I dropped down on one knee and held them up for a moment with two shots. The horsemen pulled in and unlimbered their own guns. The moonlight sparkled on naked steel.

Suddenly the entire world seemed to fly apart. I had had no idea that the explosion would be so great. Boulders flew away from the cliff. Rocks showered down like mortar shells.

The bright river was suddenly obliterated by the fog of dust and flying fragments.

I was knocked flat by the concussion. My face in the dirt, I heard the whole cliff begin to slide away.

My ears ached with the impacts of sound.

The opposing cliff caved in, jolted to its very base.

Then everything became still. The dust settled slowly and evenly over the gorge. Once more the moon shone through.

I heard a laugh behind me and scrambled up. Montrey stood there, feet spread apart, his rifle centered on my chest.

"That," said Montrey, "was very clever, *mon corporal*. And it will save me a great deal of bother. Those people cannot get out of that valley. When we came down we had to slide like goats. The upper gorge is a torrent." He pointed to the river below us.

It had ceased to run! The cliff had dammed it!

"And I suppose," I said, "that I'm to die now."

"Correct," replied Montrey, raising his Lebel the fraction of an inch which centered it on my heart. "There is no need to share that wealth with you."

I found courage enough to laugh.

"Then fire away. I still have a stick of dynamite in my pack and a box of caps to go with it. One jar and we'll both die!"

Montrey's mouth gaped. He drew hastily away from me.

"That's not far enough," I told him. "It might blow the cliff down on your head."

He backed up once more, never taking his eyes from me. When he had reached the range of fifty yards he stopped and threw the gun to his shoulder.

I dived away into the protection of an overhanging ledge. Montrey fired but he had neglected, as Ivan had neglected with the machine gun, to set his sights.

My own Lebel's crack brought the echoes out of the rocks. I fired three times. The first struck Montrey in the chest. The second and third smashed his face. He wilted toward the edge and then stumbled. His body fell into a pool of quiet water below.

Perhaps Montrey has found out in some other world that I had not possessed so much as a single cap or stick in my haversack.

I made my way to Casablanca without much difficulty, traveling fast and by night, using the stars for a compass.

Outside of that city I found a clothier and I outfitted myself, discarding Legion garb.

It was obvious that I could not go back to Sidi. One cannot readily explain the loss of an entire squad. And if I had gone back they might have given me some time with the Zephyrs just to show me that an insignificant corporal should not take the initiative of leaving his post, lack of water and temper of men notwithstanding.

Besides, *mes amis,* what need have I for a *sou* a day? Or for the cover the Legion affords to the indiscreet? I paid up my bills, paid them double—and I did not miss the price!

Story Preview

Story Preview

NOW that you've just ventured through some of the captivating tales in the Stories from the Golden Age collection by L. Ron Hubbard, turn the page and enjoy a preview of *While Bugles Blow!* Join an American Lieutenant in the French Foreign Legion caught in the middle of an ancient feud between two tribes in the Moroccan city of Harj. When a gorgeous woman finds herself drawn dangerously into the midst of the conflict, the Lieutenant does what any man must—he saves her . . . igniting a war.

While Bugles Blow!

A N offer came from the crowd.

The girl, standing there stripped before this barrage of eyes, hung her head. Her hair was long and brown and fell so as to partly hide her delicately featured face. Her eyes, blacked with kohl, flicked upward every few seconds to look at the men who bid for her.

"A rotten shame," thought the Lieutenant.

Offers were buffeted about. The auctioneer bellowed and roared, told funny stories, extolled the virtues of Jeppa women and finally brought a bidder up to a good price.

The money was paid on the spot. The big-chested, hairy-faced Berber took his merchandise. The girl, to the Lieutenant's surprise, went willingly enough.

"And now!" cried the auctioneer. "We have the best of the lot. I have here a jewel, a flame-colored flower, worth a sultan's ransom. Untouched, pure as spring water, brought up in the harem, the very harem of Kirzigh himself. She is the finest of all. When she looks at you, you think two moons have risen. When she sighs you think the gentle breezes have cooled your brows. When she talks you think that nightingales have swarmed down from the heavens. She is a gift of Allah, more beautiful than the houris themselves. Her waist could be encircled with the smallest hand. A glimpse of her face and figure would pull a dead man from his shroud. And her hair! It is the color of the dawn, of the evening. It is the color of silk beyond value. It is a crown of molten gold flowing across her milk white shoulders. My brothers, gaze upon this woman and be confounded!"

He threw back a drape, dramatically bringing forth another article.

The Lieutenant had, until now, thought that this was just some pat speech of the auctioneer's. The Lieutenant had seen many, many Arab and Berber women. Some of them were very pretty, yes, but not like this one.

My God, no!

She was all the auctioneer said and more, and the Lieutenant began to think poorly of the auctioneer's oratorical abilities.

She was beautiful, but the mention of it made that word pale and insipid.

In all his life, in magazines, on the screen, the Lieutenant had never beheld such a face or such a figure.

Her hair was golden red, her eyes were clear and alive and gray. She looked down into the crowd as though she gazed upon so many mangy camels.

The crowd said not a word. Not one man there breathed for the space of a dozen heartbeats.

Suddenly an engulfing roar soared skyward. They slapped each other and slapped themselves and laughed and cheered and howled with pleasure.

The auctioneer, conscious that he had done something great, puffed up considerably, stroked his beard and waited for them to grow quiet.

The girl was haughty and unafraid. It was her voice which struck the crowd into silence.

"What one among you dares make a bid for Morgiana, Buddir al Buddor, daughter of the Caid?"

They gaped at her. Never in the history of Harj had a woman captive had the courage to speak from the auction block.

"Why don't you bid?" she cried. "Look at me. I am beautiful. I am worth ten thousand pieces of gold. Buy me as you buy a camel or a barb. Bid, beasts, and show me which one among you wants me the most."

For seconds nothing sounded but the clattering of palms in the public square. Then a stately Berber stepped forward and cried, "One hundred pieces of gold I bid for the honor of breaking that woman's spirit."

Another voice roared, "Two hundred pieces of gold."

A third cried, "Three hundred."

The first bidder, stroking his beard, looked up at the girl thoughtfully.

She called to him. "Am I not worth it? Will you not bid five hundred, you malformed ox? Bid and show them, and then I'll show you which one of us is broken first."

The Lieutenant was still dazed. His heart was beating queerly and gave little bumps every time her white teeth flashed. Then he tried to catch hold of himself. This was no way for the conqueror of Harj to act. No way at all.

He felt something press against his side. His fingers closed on a terrific weight. He glanced down.

Just as though some spirit had come to him unseen and

had departed without noise, he found himself possessed of a big sack. It jingled.

"Bid!" cried the girl. "Buy me for a bargain at ten thousand pieces of gold. Ah, you're afraid. Afraid I might tear your eyes out of your heads and pluck your beards, hair by hair. We'll see about that. Bid!"

The Lieutenant raised the bag to shoulder height. The auctioneer stared blankly at him and at the sack.

The Lieutenant threw the money to the block. The bag broke and gold scattered over it like a torrent of sunlight.

The auctioneer's helpers dashed forward and scooped up the wealth. To their practiced eyes, it amounted to some seven or eight hundred pieces of gold.

The crowd cheered. In the middle of a nightmare, the Lieutenant stepped up, took the girl's hand in his own and tried to pull her away with him.

She stood where she was. He touched her again and their eyes met and clashed.

Suddenly she seized his hand, jerked it toward her and sank her teeth in it to the bone.

The sudden pain of it made the Lieutenant strike. The girl reeled back, dropping his hand. He looked down at the flowing blood. A stain as red as his own was against the girl's cheek.

In Shilha, the Lieutenant said, "Come with me."

She withdrew a little farther, head erect, glaring, drawing the cloak the auctioneer had handed her tightly about her white body.

The Lieutenant knew he was acting a fool. The girl hated him and, suddenly, he hated the girl.

In a voice as hard as Toledo steel, he said, "Come with me or stay where you are. I care very little what you do. I bought you with no intention of giving you anything but your liberty. You can stay here and be damned!"

He about-faced, started down. The crowd opened a path for him.

Heels ringing on the stones, he went across the square and turned down a side street, heading back for the fort.

He stopped and looked back.

The girl was ten feet behind him and they were, for the moment, alone.

Nothing had altered in her manner. She was merely following him because she could do nothing else.

"Walk beside me, if you'll walk at all," said the Lieutenant, harshly.

"Slaves," she said, "always follow at a respectful distance." Her voice purred in a deadly way. "Lead on, my master."

To find out more about *While Bugles Blow!* and how you can obtain your copy, go to www.goldenagestories.com.

Glossary

Glossary

STORIES FROM THE GOLDEN AGE *reflect the words and expressions used in the 1930s and 1940s, adding unique flavor and authenticity to the tales. While a character's speech may often reflect regional origins, it also can convey attitudes common in the day. So that readers can better grasp such cultural and historical terms, uncommon words or expressions of the era, the following glossary has been provided.*

alidade: a topographic surveying and mapping instrument used for determining directions, consisting of a telescope and attached parts.

altimeter: a gauge that measures altitude.

Atlas: Atlas Mountains; a mountain range in northwest Africa extending about fifteen hundred miles through Morocco, Algeria and Tunisia, including the Rock of Gibraltar. The Atlas ranges separate the Mediterranean and Atlantic coastlines from the Sahara Desert.

azimuth: in artillery, the angle of deviation of a projectile or bomb from a known direction, such as north or south.

bandoliers: broad belts worn over the shoulder by soldiers and having a number of small loops or pockets, for holding cartridges.

bataillon pénal: (French) penal battalion; military unit consisting of convicted persons for whom military service was either assigned punishment or a voluntary replacement of imprisonment. Penal battalion service was very dangerous: the official view was that they were highly expendable and were to be used to reduce losses in regular units. The term of service in penal units was from one to three months. Convicts were released earlier if they suffered a combat injury (the crime was considered to be "washed out with blood") or performed a heroic deed.

Berbers: members of a group of North African tribes, primarily Muslim people, living in settled or nomadic tribes between the Sahara and Mediterranean Sea, and between Egypt and the Atlantic Ocean.

burnoose: a long hooded cloak worn by some Arabs.

cafard: (French) a mood of madness and suicidal depression that commonly afflicted Legionnaires.

caid: a Berber chieftain.

cantle: the raised back part of a saddle for a horse.

Casablanca: a seaport on the Atlantic coast of Morocco.

Caudron: airplane made by the Caudron Airplane Company, a French aircraft company founded in 1909 by Gaston (1882–1915) and René (1884–1959) Caudron. It was one of the earliest aircraft manufacturers in France and produced planes for the military in both World War I and World War II.

Chauchat: a light machine-gun used mainly by the French Army. It was among the first light machine-gun designs of the early 1900s. It set a precedent for twentieth century firearm projects as it could be built inexpensively in very large numbers.

coyote: used for a man who has the sneaking and skulking characteristics of a coyote.

deuce, what the: what the devil; expressing surprise.

djellaba: a long loose hooded garment with full sleeves, worn especially in Muslim countries.

drome: short for airdrome; a military air base.

Fez: the former capital of several dynasties and one of the holiest places in Morocco; it has kept its religious primacy through the ages.

flintlock: a type of gun fired by a spark from a flint (rock used with steel to produce an igniting spark). It was introduced about 1630.

Foreign Legion: French Foreign Legion; a unique elite unit within the French Army established in 1831. It was created as a unit for foreign volunteers and was primarily used to protect and expand the French colonial empire during the nineteenth century, but has also taken part in all of France's wars with other European powers. It is known to be an elite military unit whose training focuses not only on traditional military skills, but also on the building of a strong "esprit de corps" amongst members. As its men come from different countries with different cultures, this is a widely accepted solution to strengthen them enough to work as a team. Training is often not only physically hard with brutal training methods, but also extremely stressful with high rates of desertion.

Franzawi: (Arabic) Frenchman.

G-men: government men; agents of the Federal Bureau of Investigation.

hein?: (French) eh?

High Atlas: portion of the Atlas Mountain range which rises in the west at the Atlantic coast and stretches in an eastern direction to the Moroccan-Algerian border.

houris: in Muslim belief, any of the dark-eyed virgins of perfect beauty believed to live with the blessed in Paradise.

hp: horsepower.

ifrīts: (Arabic) powerful evil *jinn*, demons or monstrous giants in Arabic mythology.

Jebel Druses: *Jebel* is Arabic for *mountain*. The *Druse* (also *Druze*) are members of a tightly organized, independent religious sect dwelling in the Jebel Druze State, a region in southern Syria named after the Jabal el Druze mountain and formerly part of the Turkish Empire. They have been known to be strong fighting people.

kepi: a cap with a circular top and a nearly horizontal visor; a French military cap that men in the Foreign Legion wear.

kohl: a cosmetic preparation used especially in the Middle East to darken the rims of the eyelids.

la Légion: (French) the Legion; the French Foreign Legion.

Lawrence: Lieutenant Colonel Thomas Edward Lawrence, also known as T. E. Lawrence. A British Army officer renowned especially for his liaison role during the Arab Revolt against the Ottoman Turkish rule of 1916–18. Extraordinary breadth and variety of his activities and associations, and his ability to describe them vividly in writing, earned him international fame as Lawrence of Arabia, a title which was used for the 1962 film based on his World War I activities. Lawrence's major written work is *Seven Pillars of Wisdom*. In addition to being a memoir of his war experience, certain parts also serve as essays on military strategy, Arabian culture and geography.

Lebels: French rifles that were adopted as standard infantry weapons in 1887 and remained in official service until after World War II.

Legion: French Foreign Legion, a specialized military unit of the French army, consisting of volunteers of all nationalities assigned to military operations and duties outside France.

Legionnaire: a member of the French Foreign Legion.

light out: to leave quickly; depart hurriedly.

lucre: money, wealth or profit.

mailed fist: superior force.

Makhzan: (Arabic) the privileged people from whom the Moroccan state officials are recruited.

Mannlicher: a type of rifle equipped with a manually operated sliding bolt that loads cartridges for firing. Ferdinand Mannlicher, an Austrian engineer and armaments designer, created rifles that were considered reasonably strong and accurate.

mes amis: (French) my friends.

mon Dieu: (French) my God.

Moorish barb: a desert horse of a breed introduced by the Moors (Muslim people of mixed Berber and Arab descent) that resembles the Arabian horse and is known for speed and endurance.

Moors: members of a northwest African Muslim people of mixed descent.

Morocco: a country of northwest Africa on the Mediterranean Sea and the Atlantic Ocean. The French established a protectorate over most of the region in 1912, and in 1956 Morocco achieved independence as a kingdom.

m'sieu: (French) sir.

Mt. Tizi-n-Tamjurt: the highest elevation in the Atlas Mountain range.

murette: (French) a low wall.

musette: a small canvas or leather bag with a shoulder strap, as one used by soldiers or travelers.

paquetage: (French) soldier's pack.

prop wash: the disturbed air pushed aft by the propeller of an aircraft.

Riffs: members of any of several Berber people inhabiting the Er Rif, a hilly region along the coast of northern Morocco. The Berber people of the area remained fiercely independent until they were subdued by French and Spanish forces (1925–1926).

Scheherazade: the female narrator of *The Arabian Nights,* who during one thousand and one adventurous nights saved her life by entertaining her husband, the king, with stories.

scow: an old or clumsy boat; hulk; tub.

Shilha: the Berber dialect spoken in the mountains of southern Morocco.

sīdī: (Arabic) my lord.

Sidi-bel-Abbès: the capital of the Sidi-bel-Abbès province in Algeria. The city was developed around a French camp built in 1843. From 1931 until 1961, the city was the "holy city" or spiritual home of the French Foreign Legion, the location of its basic training camp and the headquarters of its first foreign regiment.

Snider: a rifle formerly used in the British service. It was invented by American Jacob Snider in the mid-1800s. The Snider was a breech-loading rifle, derived from its muzzle-loading predecessor called the Enfield.

sou: (French) a French coin worth a very small amount.

Toledo: Toledo, Spain; a city renowned for making swords of finely tempered steel.

turtleback: the part of the airplane behind the cockpit that is shaped like the back of a turtle.

Zephyrs: penal battalions for the French Foreign Legion; nickname given in Algeria to a corps which is recruited from the French Army, those who would not conform to discipline or who were criminals. This punishment, no matter its length, does not count in the term of military duty which the state requires.

L. Ron Hubbard
in the Golden Age
of Pulp Fiction

*In writing an adventure story
a writer has to know that he is adventuring
for a lot of people who cannot.
The writer has to take them here and there
about the globe and show them
excitement and love and realism.
As long as that writer is living the part of an
adventurer when he is hammering
the keys, he is succeeding with his story.*

*Adventuring is a state of mind.
If you adventure through life, you have a
good chance to be a success on paper.*

*Adventure doesn't mean globe-trotting,
exactly, and it doesn't mean great deeds.
Adventuring is like art.
You have to live it to make it real.*

— *L. RON HUBBARD*

L. Ron Hubbard and American Pulp Fiction

B ORN March 13, 1911, L. Ron Hubbard lived a life at least as expansive as the stories with which he enthralled a hundred million readers through a fifty-year career.

Originally hailing from Tilden, Nebraska, he spent his formative years in a classically rugged Montana, replete with the cowpunchers, lawmen and desperadoes who would later people his Wild West adventures. And lest anyone imagine those adventures were drawn from vicarious experience, he was not only breaking broncs at a tender age, he was also among the few whites ever admitted into Blackfoot society as a bona fide blood brother. While if only to round out an otherwise rough and tumble youth, his mother was that rarity of her time—a thoroughly educated woman—who introduced her son to the classics of Occidental literature even before his seventh birthday.

But as any dedicated L. Ron Hubbard reader will attest, his world extended far beyond Montana. In point of fact, and as the son of a United States naval officer, by the age of eighteen he had traveled over a quarter of a million miles. Included therein were three Pacific crossings to a then still mysterious Asia, where he ran with the likes of Her British Majesty's agent-in-place

for North China, and the last in the line of Royal Magicians from the court of Kublai Khan. For the record, L. Ron Hubbard was also among the first Westerners to gain admittance to forbidden Tibetan monasteries below Manchuria, and his photographs of China's Great Wall long graced American geography texts.

L. Ron Hubbard, left, at Congressional Airport, Washington, DC, 1931, with members of George Washington University flying club.

Upon his return to the United States and a hasty completion of his interrupted high school education, the young Ron Hubbard entered George Washington University. There, as fans of his aerial adventures may have heard, he earned his wings as a pioneering barnstormer at the dawn of American aviation. He also earned a place in free-flight record books for the longest sustained flight above Chicago. Moreover, as a roving reporter for *Sportsman Pilot* (featuring his first professionally penned articles), he further helped inspire a generation of pilots who would take America to world airpower.

Immediately beyond his sophomore year, Ron embarked on the first of his famed ethnological expeditions, initially to then untrammeled Caribbean shores (descriptions of which would later fill a whole series of West Indies mystery-thrillers). That the Puerto Rican interior would also figure into the future of Ron Hubbard stories was likewise no accident. For in addition to cultural studies of the island, a 1932–33

LRH expedition is rightly remembered as conducting the first complete mineralogical survey of a Puerto Rico under United States jurisdiction.

There was many another adventure along this vein: As a lifetime member of the famed Explorers Club, L. Ron Hubbard charted North Pacific waters with the first shipboard radio direction finder, and so pioneered a long-range navigation system universally employed until the late twentieth century. While not to put too fine an edge on it, he also held a rare Master Mariner's license to pilot any vessel, of any tonnage in any ocean.

Yet lest we stray too far afield, there is an LRH note at this juncture in his saga, and it reads in part:

"I started out writing for the pulps, writing the best I knew, writing for every mag on the stands, slanting as well as I could."

Capt. L. Ron Hubbard in Ketchikan, Alaska, 1940, on his Alaskan Radio Experimental Expedition, the first of three voyages conducted under the Explorers Club flag.

To which one might add: His earliest submissions date from the summer of 1934, and included tales drawn from true-to-life Asian adventures, with characters roughly modeled on British/American intelligence operatives he had known in Shanghai. His early Westerns were similarly peppered with details drawn from personal experience. Although therein lay a first hard lesson from the often cruel world of the pulps. His first Westerns were soundly rejected as lacking the authenticity of a Max Brand yarn (a particularly frustrating comment given L. Ron Hubbard's Westerns came straight from his Montana homeland, while Max Brand was a mediocre New York poet named Frederick Schiller Faust, who turned out implausible six-shooter tales from the terrace of an Italian villa).

Nevertheless, and needless to say, L. Ron Hubbard persevered and soon earned a reputation as among the most publishable names in pulp fiction, with a ninety percent placement rate of first-draft manuscripts. He was also among the most prolific, averaging between seventy and a hundred thousand words a month. Hence the rumors that L. Ron Hubbard had redesigned a typewriter for faster keyboard action and pounded out manuscripts on a continuous roll of butcher paper to save the precious seconds it took to insert a single sheet of paper into manual typewriters of the day.

That all L. Ron Hubbard stories did not run beneath said byline is yet another aspect of pulp fiction lore. That is, as publishers periodically rejected manuscripts from top-drawer authors if only to avoid paying top dollar, L. Ron Hubbard and company just as frequently replied with submissions under various pseudonyms. In Ron's case, the

A MAN OF MANY NAMES

Between 1934 and 1950, L. Ron Hubbard authored more than fifteen million words of fiction in more than two hundred classic publications. To supply his fans and editors with stories across an array of genres and pulp titles, he adopted fifteen pseudonyms in addition to his already renowned L. Ron Hubbard byline.

Winchester Remington Colt
Lt. Jonathan Daly
Capt. Charles Gordon
Capt. L. Ron Hubbard
Bernard Hubbel
Michael Keith
Rene Lafayette
Legionnaire 148
Legionnaire 14830
Ken Martin
Scott Morgan
Lt. Scott Morgan
Kurt von Rachen
Barry Randolph
Capt. Humbert Reynolds

list included: Rene Lafayette, Captain Charles Gordon, Lt. Scott Morgan and the notorious Kurt von Rachen—supposedly on the lam for a murder rap, while hammering out two-fisted prose in Argentina. The point: While L. Ron Hubbard as Ken Martin spun stories of Southeast Asian intrigue, LRH as Barry Randolph authored tales of

romance on the Western range—which, stretching between a dozen genres is how he came to stand among the two hundred elite authors providing close to a million tales through the glory days of American Pulp Fiction.

L. Ron Hubbard, circa 1930, at the outset of a literary career that would finally span half a century.

In evidence of exactly that, by 1936 L. Ron Hubbard was literally leading pulp fiction's elite as president of New York's American Fiction Guild. Members included a veritable pulp hall of fame: Lester "Doc Savage" Dent, Walter "The Shadow" Gibson, and the legendary Dashiell Hammett—to cite but a few.

Also in evidence of just where L. Ron Hubbard stood within his first two years on the American pulp circuit: By the spring of 1937, he was ensconced in Hollywood, adopting a Caribbean thriller for Columbia Pictures, remembered today as *The Secret of Treasure Island*. Comprising fifteen thirty-minute episodes, the L. Ron Hubbard screenplay led to the most profitable matinée serial in Hollywood history. In accord with Hollywood culture, he was thereafter continually called upon

The 1937 Secret of Treasure Island, *a fifteen-episode serial adapted for the screen by L. Ron Hubbard from his novel,* Murder at Pirate Castle.

to rewrite/doctor scripts—most famously for long-time friend and fellow adventurer Clark Gable.

In the interim—and herein lies another distinctive chapter of the L. Ron Hubbard story—he continually worked to open Pulp Kingdom gates to up-and-coming authors. Or, for that matter, anyone who wished to write. It was a fairly unconventional stance, as markets were already thin and competition razor sharp. But the fact remains, it was an L. Ron Hubbard hallmark that he vehemently lobbied on behalf of young authors—regularly supplying instructional articles to trade journals, guest-lecturing to short story classes at George Washington University and Harvard, and even founding his own creative writing competition. It was established in 1940, dubbed the Golden Pen, and guaranteed winners both New York representation and publication in *Argosy*.

But it was John W. Campbell Jr.'s *Astounding Science Fiction* that finally proved the most memorable LRH vehicle. While every fan of L. Ron Hubbard's galactic epics undoubtedly knows the story, it nonetheless bears repeating: By late 1938, the pulp publishing magnate of Street & Smith was determined to revamp *Astounding Science Fiction* for broader readership. In particular, senior editorial director F. Orlin Tremaine called for stories with a stronger *human element*. When acting editor John W. Campbell balked, preferring his spaceship-driven tales, Tremaine enlisted Hubbard. Hubbard, in turn, replied with the genre's first truly *character-driven* works, wherein heroes are pitted not against bug-eyed monsters but the mystery and majesty of deep space itself—and thus was launched the Golden Age of Science Fiction.

The names alone are enough to quicken the pulse of any science fiction aficionado, including LRH friend and protégé, Robert Heinlein, Isaac Asimov, A. E. van Vogt and Ray Bradbury. Moreover, when coupled with LRH stories of fantasy, we further come to what's rightly been described as the

foundation of every modern tale of horror: L. Ron Hubbard's immortal *Fear*. It was rightly proclaimed by Stephen King as one of the very few works to genuinely warrant that overworked term "classic"—as in: *"This is a classic tale of creeping, surreal menace and horror. . . . This is one of the really, really good ones."*

L. Ron Hubbard, 1948, among fellow science fiction luminaries at the World Science Fiction Convention in Toronto.

To accommodate the greater body of L. Ron Hubbard fantasies, Street & Smith inaugurated *Unknown*—a classic pulp if there ever was one, and wherein readers were soon thrilling to the likes of *Typewriter in the Sky* and *Slaves of Sleep* of which Frederik Pohl would declare: *"There are bits and pieces from Ron's work that became part of the language in ways that very few other writers managed."*

And, indeed, at J. W. Campbell Jr.'s insistence, Ron was regularly drawing on themes from the Arabian Nights and so introducing readers to a world of genies, jinn, Aladdin and Sinbad—all of which, of course, continue to float through cultural mythology to this day.

At least as influential in terms of post-apocalypse stories was L. Ron Hubbard's 1940 *Final Blackout*. Generally acclaimed as the finest anti-war novel of the decade and among the ten best works of the genre ever authored—here, too, was a tale that would live on in ways few other writers imagined.

Portland, Oregon, 1943; L. Ron Hubbard, captain of the US Navy subchaser PC 815.

Hence, the later Robert Heinlein verdict: "Final Blackout *is as perfect a piece of science fiction as has ever been written.*"

Like many another who both lived and wrote American pulp adventure, the war proved a tragic end to Ron's sojourn in the pulps. He served with distinction in four theaters and was highly decorated for commanding corvettes in the North Pacific. He was also grievously wounded in combat, lost many a close friend and colleague and thus resolved to say farewell to pulp fiction and devote himself to what it had supported these many years—namely, his serious research.

But in no way was the LRH literary saga at an end, for as he wrote some thirty years later, in 1980:

"Recently there came a period when I had little to do. This was novel in a life so crammed with busy years, and I decided to amuse myself by writing a novel that was pure *science fiction."*

That work was *Battlefield Earth: A Saga of the Year 3000*. It was an immediate *New York Times* bestseller and, in fact, the first international science fiction blockbuster in decades. It was not, however, L. Ron Hubbard's magnum opus, as that distinction is generally reserved for his next and final work: The 1.2 million word *Mission Earth*.

> **Final Blackout**
> *is as perfect*
> *a piece of*
> *science fiction*
> *as has ever*
> *been written.*
>
> —Robert Heinlein

How he managed those 1.2 million words in just over twelve months is yet another piece of the L. Ron Hubbard legend. But the fact remains, he did indeed author a ten-volume *dekalogy* that lives in publishing history for the fact that each and every volume of the series was also a *New York Times* bestseller.

Moreover, as subsequent generations discovered L. Ron Hubbard through republished works and novelizations of his screenplays, the mere fact of his name on a cover signaled an international bestseller. . . . Until, to date, sales of his works exceed hundreds of millions, and he otherwise remains among the most enduring and widely read authors in literary history. Although as a final word on the tales of L. Ron Hubbard, perhaps it's enough to simply reiterate what editors told readers in the glory days of American Pulp Fiction:

He writes the way he does, brothers, because he's been there, seen it and done it!

THE STORIES FROM THE GOLDEN AGE

Your ticket to adventure starts here with the Stories from
the Golden Age collection by master storyteller L. Ron Hubbard.
These gripping tales are set in a kaleidoscope of exotic locales and brim
with fascinating characters, including some of the
most vile villains, dangerous dames and brazen heroes
you'll ever get to meet.

The entire collection of over one hundred and fifty stories is being
released in a series of eighty books and audiobooks.
For an up-to-date listing of available titles,
go to www.goldenagestories.com.

AIR ADVENTURE

Arctic Wings	*Man-Killers of the Air*
The Battling Pilot	*On Blazing Wings*
Boomerang Bomber	*Red Death Over China*
The Crate Killer	*Sabotage in the Sky*
The Dive Bomber	*Sky Birds Dare!*
Forbidden Gold	*The Sky-Crasher*
Hurtling Wings	*Trouble on His Wings*
The Lieutenant Takes the Sky	*Wings Over Ethiopia*

FAR-FLUNG ADVENTURE

The Adventure of "X"	*Hurricane*
All Frontiers Are Jealous	*The Iron Duke*
The Barbarians	*Machine Gun 21,000*
The Black Sultan	*Medals for Mahoney*
Black Towers to Danger	*Price of a Hat*
The Bold Dare All	*Red Sand*
Buckley Plays a Hunch	*The Sky Devil*
The Cossack	*The Small Boss of Nunaloha*
Destiny's Drum	*The Squad That Never Came Back*
Escape for Three	*Starch and Stripes*
Fifty-Fifty O'Brien	*Tomb of the Ten Thousand Dead*
The Headhunters	*Trick Soldier*
Hell's Legionnaire	*While Bugles Blow!*
He Walked to War	*Yukon Madness*
Hostage to Death	

SEA ADVENTURE

Cargo of Coffins	*The Phantom Patrol*
The Drowned City	*Sea Fangs*
False Cargo	*Submarine*
Grounded	*Twenty Fathoms Down*
Loot of the Shanung	*Under the Black Ensign*
Mister Tidwell, Gunner	

TALES FROM THE ORIENT

The Devil—With Wings   *Pearl Pirate*
The Falcon Killer   *The Red Dragon*
Five Mex for a Million   *Spy Killer*
Golden Hell   *Tah*
The Green God   *The Trail of the Red Diamonds*
Hurricane's Roar   *Wind-Gone-Mad*
Inky Odds   *Yellow Loot*
Orders Is Orders

MYSTERY

The Blow Torch Murder   *The Grease Spot*
Brass Keys to Murder   *Killer Ape*
Calling Squad Cars!   *Killer's Law*
The Carnival of Death   *The Mad Dog Murder*
The Chee-Chalker   *Mouthpiece*
Dead Men Kill   *Murder Afloat*
The Death Flyer   *The Slickers*
Flame City   *They Killed Him Dead*

FANTASY

Borrowed Glory	*If I Were You*
The Crossroads	*The Last Drop*
Danger in the Dark	*The Room*
The Devil's Rescue	*The Tramp*
He Didn't Like Cats	

SCIENCE FICTION

The Automagic Horse	*A Matter of Matter*
Battle of Wizards	*The Obsolete Weapon*
Battling Bolto	*One Was Stubborn*
The Beast	*The Planet Makers*
Beyond All Weapons	*The Professor Was a Thief*
A Can of Vacuum	*The Slaver*
The Conroy Diary	*Space Can*
The Dangerous Dimension	*Strain*
Final Enemy	*Tough Old Man*
The Great Secret	*240,000 Miles Straight Up*
Greed	*When Shadows Fall*
The Invaders	

WESTERN

The Baron of Coyote River   Man for Breakfast
Blood on His Spurs   The No-Gun Gunhawk
Boss of the Lazy B   The No-Gun Man
Branded Outlaw   The Ranch That No One Would Buy
Cattle King for a Day   Reign of the Gila Monster
Come and Get It   Ride 'Em, Cowboy
Death Waits at Sundown   Ruin at Rio Piedras
Devil's Manhunt   Shadows from Boot Hill
The Ghost Town Gun-Ghost   Silent Pards
Gun Boss of Tumbleweed   Six-Gun Caballero
Gunman!   Stacked Bullets
Gunman's Tally   Stranger in Town
The Gunner from Gehenna   Tinhorn's Daughter
Hoss Tamer   The Toughest Ranger
Johnny, the Town Tamer   Under the Diehard Brand
King of the Gunmen   Vengeance Is Mine!
The Magic Quirt   When Gilhooly Was in Flower

Engage the Legions Under the Banner of Excitement!

An American lieutenant in the French Foreign Legion is caught in the middle of an ancient feud between the Jeppas of the Atlas Mountains and the bloodthirsty tribe of Perviz al Bahman.

Tension mounts as a gorgeous female Jeppa warrior with golden red hair is drawn into the midst of the conflict and captured by Perviz's tribe. When the American lieutenant later finds her being sold on the slave market, he unthinkingly does what any man must: he rescues her. But while his actions may have saved a beauty, they have also just ignited all-out war.

Get
While Bugles Blow!

PAPERBACK OR AUDIOBOOK: **$9.95** EACH
Free Shipping & Handling for Book Club Members
CALL TOLL-FREE: 1-877-8GALAXY (1-877-842-5299)
OR GO ONLINE TO **www.goldenagestories.com**

Galaxy Press, 7051 Hollywood Blvd., Suite 200, Hollywood, CA 90028

JOIN THE PULP REVIVAL
America in the 1930s and 40s

Pulp fiction was in its heyday and 30 million readers were regularly riveted by the larger-than-life tales of master storyteller L. Ron Hubbard. For this was pulp fiction's golden age, when the writing was raw and every page packed a walloping punch.

That magic can now be yours. An evocative world of nefarious villains, exotic intrigues, courageous heroes and heroines—a world that today's cinema has barely tapped for tales of adventure and swashbucklers.

Enroll today in the Stories from the Golden Age Club and begin receiving your monthly feature edition selected from more than 150 stories in the collection.

You may choose to enjoy them as either a paperback or audiobook for the special membership price of $9.95 each month along with FREE shipping and handling.

CALL TOLL-FREE: **1-877-8GALAXY**
(1-877-842-5299) OR GO ONLINE TO
www.goldenagestories.com
AND BECOME PART OF THE PULP REVIVAL!